PRAISE FOR
YOLO

Booklist:
★ This honest, nuanced, accessible, and credible
account provides teen girls with an authentic and
skillfully told description of college life.

Kirkus Reviews:
Funny, deceptively smart and just in time
for those going off to college.

PRAISE & ACCOLADES FOR
THE INTERNET GIRLS SERIES

New York Times bestselling series
San Francisco Chronicle bestselling series
Publishers Weekly bestselling series

School Library Journal:
★ Both revealing and innovative, this novel will
inspire teens to pass it to their friends . . . nonnarrative
communication can be a great way to tell a story.

LAUREN MYRACLE

yolo

AMULET BOOKS · NEW YORK

The Library of Congress has catalogued the hardcover edition of this book as follows:

Myracle, Lauren, 1969–
Yolo / Lauren Myracle.
pages cm — (Internet girls, the)
ISBN 978-1-4197-0871-8 (hardback) —
ISBN 978-1-61312-504-5 (ebook)
[1. Instant messaging—Fiction. 2. Best friends—Fiction. 3. Friendship—Fiction. 4. Interpersonal relations—Fiction. 5. Colleges and universities—Fiction.] I. Title. II. Title: You only live once.
PZ7.M9955Yol 2014
[Fic]—dc23
2014014986

ISBN for this edition: 978-1-4197-1665-2

Text copyright © 2014 Lauren Myracle
Book design by Maria T. Middleton

Printed and bound in U.S.A.
10 9 8 7 6 5 4 3 2 1

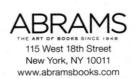
ABRAMS
THE ART OF BOOKS SINCE 1949
115 West 18th Street
New York, NY 10011
www.abramsbooks.com

To AI, who is fantastic

mad maddie: YO, ANGELA, I'VE JOINED THE COLLEGE GIRL RANKS AT LAST! 😳

mad maddie: do I get my special beret now?

SnowAngel: Maddie! my Cali girl! 💣

SnowAngel: rock on, UC Santa Cruz. you so smexy!

mad maddie: girl, I will hit you on the head with a frying pan if you call me smexy. gross! boo!

mad maddie: but. California. SO FRICKIN GORGEOUS.

mad maddie: the sky is so blue and the forest is everywhere and there is sunshine sunshine sunshine, and I LOVE IT.

SnowAngel: we have the sky and the sun in Georgia too, dum-dum. and! omg! we also have 🌲 🌲 🌲 s!

mad maddie: is different here. is stunning. so are the students, as apparently it is the law that all California kids must have good genes. I might have to dye my hair blond.

SnowAngel: yr hair is already blond

mad maddie: eh, fair enough

SnowAngel: so weird that yr JUST NOW starting the semester. do you realize that I've been at UGA for over a month? and that Zoe's been at Kenyon for almost as long???

mad maddie: why, yes, Angela, I do realize that.

mad maddie: do you think I've lived in a time bubble for the last four weeks? do you think I wanted to stay in Atlanta—IN MY PARENTS' HOUSE, WITH MY PARENTS WHO STILL USE TV TRAYS SO THEY CAN EAT TOTINO'S FROZEN PIZZA WHILE WATCHING "FAMILY GUY"—while you and Z were off having Adventure Time in your sparkly new lives?

SnowAngel: aw, now. I'm sure yr parents heat up the pizza before eating it, silly.

mad maddie: you'd be surprised

SnowAngel: but seriously. it's like Zoe and I are college grads, practically, while you're still a wee freshman. *pats wee Maddie on her blondie head* *uses wee voice* look at you, wearing yr big girl college beret!

mad maddie: hey, you need to be nice to me. the flight to California was five hours long—and the whole time I was strapped in next to a man who watched episode after episode of "House Hunters" on his tablet WITHOUT HEADPHONES.

SnowAngel: "House Hunters" normal or "House Hunters International"?

mad maddie: he was on a plane full of other ppl. how cld he not know to wear headphones? I kept wanting to say something to him, but I didn't. and then I kept hoping that one of the flight attendants wld say something to him, but none of them did! ever!!!

SnowAngel: I like "House Hunters," even tho the couple already knows which house they're going to buy before the show is filmed. did u know that?

mad maddie: nope, and while I love you, I don't really care.

mad maddie: but I did some thinking on my long-ass flight and I had a very brilliant realization that I wld like to share with you. 💡

mad maddie: you know the expression "you only live once"?

SnowAngel: as in yolo? *lifts eyebrows*

SnowAngel: no, never heard of it. just like the ten-year-old my sister babysits has never heard of it, and just like my *grandmother* has never heard of it.

mad maddie: har har har

mad maddie: you and me and Zoe, we've all gone our own ways and we're spread out all over the country and we're, like, growing up and shit.

SnowAngel:	"growing up and shit." You've gone all sophisticated, college girl.
mad maddie:	**but just cuz we're growing up doesn't mean we have to grow apart.**
SnowAngel:	Maddie, that's so corny! you're so adorable!!! 🌽
mad maddie:	**and with that in mind, I have a plan for keeping us together.**
SnowAngel:	does it include finishing my business hw for me? cuz shocking as it is, I wld actually NOT like to weigh in on how modern control theory is used in evaluating economic conditions.
SnowAngel:	MY BUSINESS CLASS IS SOOOOOO BORING!
mad maddie:	**I feel for you. back to what *I* was saying. I just think we shld—**
mad maddie:	**shit**
SnowAngel:	you think we should shit? 🍵
mad maddie:	**my orientation leader is calling everyone over for a group activity. I've gotta go.**
SnowAngel:	hold on. you think we shld what?
mad maddie:	**tell ya later. will call as soon as I can.**
SnowAngel:	don't use drugs! drugs make you stoopid! that's what the orientation person's going to tell you!
mad maddie:	**kk, I won't. don't u either!**

Fri, Sept 20, 7:39 PM E.D.T.

SnowAngel:	Maddie made it to California! yaaaaaay!
zoegirl:	I know, cuz I saw her pic of the UC Santa Cruz sign. 😊
zoegirl:	did you talk to her? is she thrilled to finally be there?
zoegirl:	did you tell her what's going on with me and Doug?
SnowAngel:	no, cuz she just got there.
SnowAngel:	and I'm totally not saying this to be insensitive, but

	the stuff with Doug is really just . . . well . . . more of the same, isn't it?
SnowAngel:	altho you know I am always here and that I am hugging you from . . . however many states there are b/w GA and Ohio!
SnowAngel:	hey, quick question, my smartie friend. just randomly asking, but . . . however many states *are* there b/w GA and Ohio?? ten? twelve? four and a half?
zoegirl:	**two. but you're right. let's change the subject.**
SnowAngel:	okeydoke
SnowAngel:	in that case, I will share with you that I kinda want to strangle my roommate and burn her with fire.
zoegirl:	**oh, that Lucy. what did she do now?**
SnowAngel:	to start with, I think she's stealing from me. I will save that topic for another time, however.
SnowAngel:	what I'm annoyed about right now is her bad attitude. last night we had an all-dorm BBQ, and she rolled her eyes right out of her head when everyone sang the Georgia fight song, which goes like this:
SnowAngel:	Goooooooo, Dawgs! Sic 'em! Woof, woof, woof!
zoegirl:	**huh**
zoegirl:	**wow**
SnowAngel:	it takes one's breath away. I know.
SnowAngel:	but Lucy, who as you know IS ALSO A FRESHMAN AT UGA, showed no love for the poor little Georgia Bulldogs. and then later she started an Instagram account for "UGA Haters." isn't that so tacky?
SnowAngel:	she used a pic of a confederate flag, which happens to be hanging in the window of one of the frat houses.
zoegirl:	**ew**
SnowAngel:	ew to the flag or ew to Lucy's hate page?
zoegirl:	**both**
SnowAngel:	AND she's been making snide remarks about

the Greek system in general. she thinks I'm a horrible person for joining a sorority, even tho the Alpha Zetas wld NEVER hang a confederate flag anywhere.

zoegirl: did she say that on her hate page? I hate hate pages, btw.

SnowAngel: she said that everyone who goes to Georgia is a redneck, a racist, or a beauty queen—or very possibly all three. AND she made fun of the woof-woof song.

zoegirl: 😶

SnowAngel: so explain, please: why did Lucy enroll at a school she hates?

zoegirl: state school? low tuition?

SnowAngel: 🙂

SnowAngel: unhelpful

zoegirl: yeah, well, Lucy may not be your new BFF (she better not be!), but at least you have a roommate.

SnowAngel: puh-lease. having a single is living the dream, my friend. no sympathy points there.

zoegirl: grrr. everyone says I'm soooo lucky to have gotten a single, but I don't know.

zoegirl: sometimes it's nice . . .

zoegirl: but sometimes it's lonely.

SnowAngel: I'd happily mail Lucy to you if I cld, but alas, I have yet to persuade her to climb into an envelope.

SnowAngel: as for the lonely . . .

SnowAngel: go ahead, toots. let it out. is there a new Doug installment since the awkward phone call installment?

zoegirl: no. I'm just missing him like crazy. 🙁

zoegirl: but our phone call this morning WAS awkward. something weird is definitely going on between us . . . but please don't lecture me, because I already know I'm being pathetic.

zoegirl: if Doug's going to break up with me, he's going to break up with me, right?

SnowAngel: if Doug breaks up with you, he's an idiot—and if there IS something weird going on, I'm sure it's just the whole being at different colleges thing.

zoegirl: I know, I know.

zoegirl: it is hard to not physically BE with someone. Skyping helps, and FaceTime, but it's nothing like the real thing.

SnowAngel: that might be the whole problem, you know. it's so easy to read someone's signals wrong over texts.

zoegirl: maybe

zoegirl: but this morning's weirdness DIDN'T happen over text.

zoegirl: did I tell you the part about how he interrupted me?

SnowAngel: mainly you told me that he seemed kind of distracted.

zoegirl: because he did. it made me wonder what he was distracted BY.

SnowAngel: that's the kind of thinking that'll drive you nutso

zoegirl: and then, right as I was in the middle of saying how excited I am to see him this weekend, he cut me off and said, "Zoe, you know I love you, but you don't have to come up tomorrow if you don't want to."

SnowAngel: what? why? and why didn't you tell me earlier?

zoegirl: I don't know. because I was embarrassed?

zoegirl: then he went on this spiel about "it's such a long drive, we've both got so much work, and shouldn't you be making friends at Kenyon?"

SnowAngel:	hmm
SnowAngel:	first of all, don't EVER be embarrassed to tell me anything. that is the law and you know it.
SnowAngel:	second of all, I agree that it's strange for him to tell you not to visit him, but he's kind of right about the friends thing.
SnowAngel:	he's making new friends, so shldn't you do the same thing? and then you wldn't feel so lonely!
zoegirl:	I *am* doing that!
zoegirl:	kind of
zoegirl:	I just don't like parties and loudness and being bumped into by drunk people. I always feel like such a wallflower.
SnowAngel:	but you choose to be a wallflower! if you got in there and, like, mingled, it wld be a whole diff story!
zoegirl:	whatever. it's not even a two-hour drive from Kenyon to Oberlin. doesn't he *want* me to come?
SnowAngel:	oh, sweetie, I'm sure he does.
SnowAngel:	are you still going to?
zoegirl:	yes, because I love him.
SnowAngel:	I know, but you can't spend ALL your time missing him.
zoegirl:	I don't! I'm also studying my butt off!
zoegirl:	but what if I can't help it?
SnowAngel:	you can.
zoegirl:	can I?
SnowAngel:	aaargh. you are awesome and wonderful—of course you can! 😝!!!

Fri, Sept 20, 10:39 PM P.D.T.

mad maddie:	hey, kids. are either of you awake?
mad maddie:	Zo? Angela?
mad maddie:	anyone . . . ?

mad maddie: curse this different time zone nonsense!

mad maddie: but! my plan! Zo, did Angela tell you I have a plan for the three of us?

mad maddie: if not, that's ok. I'll tell you myself. I haz a plan!

mad maddie: it came to me on the plane ride. I was reading the stuff in my orientation packet, and there was a section with advice from past students, and one of them said something like this:

mad maddie: "college is a time to experiment. your path won't always be clear, but this is your chance to figure out what you want to do with your life. don't let fear hold you back."

mad maddie: and I totally agree. don't y'all?

mad maddie: so we, the winsome threesome, are going to make a pact that we will Eat. College. Up. we gotta hit the ground dancing before the music slows down!

mad maddie: we'll try everything that comes our way, and we won't be afraid, because even tho we're spread out all over the country, we're still here to support each other.

mad maddie: I know you're probably thinking, "der, of course we'll support each other. it's a given!"

mad maddie: and it is, but I mean it in a very intentional way. like, if we ever need that extra push to try something scary, we can think to ourselves, "hey, if Angela can stick with the Business 101 course she accidentally registered for and Zoe can stand up to the girl who hogs the washing machine by leaving her wet clothes in it FOR HOURS, then surely I can [fill in the blank]."

mad maddie: yolo, baby.

mad maddie: YO.

mad maddie: LO.

mad maddie: so that's my plan, kiddos. we won't say no to a single opportunity that comes our way.

mad maddie: everyone in? if not, speak up now . . .

mad maddie: *hum of distant mini-fridge*

mad maddie: *crickets chirping*

mad maddie: *ticking of clock*

mad maddie: we all agree! YAY! here's to taking the leap!

Sat, Sept 21, 8:53 AM E.D.T.

zoegirl: hey, Maddie. I saw yr five zillion txts when I woke up this morning. you scared me—I thought something was wrong!

zoegirl: as for your plan . . .

zoegirl: I agree in theory, but I'm not *quite* sure I'm ready to commit to doing *everything* that comes my way. I'm saying that to be honest, because you know that if I make a pact, I take it seriously.

zoegirl: right now, tho, I'm about to take off to see Doug and I need one of yr pep talks.

zoegirl: Mads?

zoegirl: oh yeah. time zone. oops.

zoegirl: well, I'll be on the road for a couple of hours, so if you wake up in time, call me. I need to know how you and Ian are handling the whole awful distance thing!!

Sat, Sept 21, 9:38 AM P.D.T.

mad maddie: hey, lady. just talked to Zoe—she's not a happy camper.

SnowAngel: is she at Oberlin? is she with Doug?

mad maddie: yes at Oberlin. not sure if she's with Doug-o. when we hung up, she was still sitting in her car in the parking lot. said her stomach hurt from nervousness.

SnowAngel: poor girl. there's something wrong if you're nervous to visit yr boyfriend, huh?

mad maddie: yeah. she told me how Doug's been pulling away, and how scared she is, and I just wanted to . . . agh. give her a Popsicle.

SnowAngel: a Popsicle, huh? cuz Popsicles always make things better? 😄

mad maddie: exactly

SnowAngel: you and Ian are dealing with the same stuff, but you don't have a nervous tummy about him, do you?

SnowAngel: btw, how IS Ian? the boy goes to the same school as me and I never see him. prolly cuz he's a GDI. 🙂

mad maddie: what's a GDI?

SnowAngel: a goddamn independent

mad maddie: a goddamn whatie-what?

SnowAngel: it means he's not a Greek. he didn't pledge a fraternity.

mad maddie: haha. can you for a single microsecond see Ian in a fraternity?

mad maddie: *gives Angela a microsecond to ponder*

mad maddie: hahahaha. thought so.

SnowAngel: whoa, you type FAST.

mad maddie: but no, Ian doesn't give me a nervous tummy (except in a good way). then again, he came and saw me off at the airport, so it's been all of two days since I've seen him.

mad maddie: then AGAIN, he's Ian. we're solid, babes.

SnowAngel: 👍

SnowAngel: and now back to me. since I am *not* a GDI, and since I'm super-cool, I'm going to a mixer tonight at the Kappa house.

SnowAngel: wanna know the theme?

mad maddie: Angela. surely you know by now that I am not a "theme" girl.

SnowAngel: it's "Can't Be Tamed." as in, ROAR! R-O-A-R!!!

mad maddie: ugh. blah. GROSS.

mad maddie: the idea of a roaring sorority girl is very disturbing and likely to give me nightmares.

SnowAngel: boom-boom-clap on yr head. 😧

SnowAngel: it's going to be fantastic. everyone gets to dress up as an animal! or a pet!

mad maddie: an animal OR a pet?

mad maddie: what kind of pet isn't an animal?

SnowAngel: *sticks out tongue*

mad maddie: ooo, I've got one. how about a louse? lice live on your head, so that makes them pets, right?

SnowAngel: no

mad maddie: Angela, it wld be MY DREAM COME TRUE if you go to your party as a louse. wld you? for me? please?

mad maddie: 🐜 🐜 🐜

SnowAngel: I'm not going to my first mixer as a louse. *pouts and puts hands on hips* I mean GOD, Maddie. like, really?

mad maddie: you're imitating a sorority girl when you ARE a sorority girl. sweet!

SnowAngel: I'm going as a 🐱

mad maddie: a kitten? really?

SnowAngel: meeee-ow!

mad maddie: HACK HACK HACK HACK HACK

mad maddie: that is the sound of me coughing up a hair ball. is it yr goal to degrade women everywhere?

SnowAngel: *licks paw* *arches back* *swishes tail sexiliciously*

mad maddie: barfing again

SnowAngel: at least I have plans. my roommate, Lucy, never has plans. ALL SHE EVER DOES IS STAY IN THE ROOM AND READ.

mad maddie: reading! in college! the horror!

SnowAngel: and when she does go out, she does weird things,
    like lurk around the dorm all skulkishly.

SnowAngel: she's also stealing my Q-tips.

mad maddie: **?**

SnowAngel: I'm not kidding. Lucy is stealing my Q-tips, and it's
    NOT cool, only I don't know how to confront her
    about it.

mad maddie: **how do you know she's stealing yr Q-tips? do you
count them?**

SnowAngel: don't judge

mad maddie: **you're my boo thang, A. I wld never.**

mad maddie: **hey—you're on board with plan yolo, right?**

SnowAngel: dude, it's college. I was never planning on NOT
    living it up. plus, you're *my* boo thang. how cld I
    say no to you?

mad maddie: **excellent. just took a screen shot so you can't go
back on yr word. byeas!**

              Sun, Sept 22, 11:56 AM E.D.T.

zoegirl: well, Mads, you were right.

mad maddie: **of course I was.**

mad maddie: **about what?**

zoegirl: about neediness turning a guy off.

zoegirl: and by a guy, I mean Doug.

zoegirl: and by neediness, I mean . . .

mad maddie: **way ahead of you, girl.**

mad maddie: **oh, Zoe. what happened? r u still at Oberlin?**

zoegirl: yeah, in Doug's dorm room. he's still sleeping.

zoegirl: as for what happened . . . arrghhh.

zoegirl: there's a girl who lives on Doug's hall named
    Canyon. Canyon—what kind of a name is that?

mad maddie: **a cool name, unfortunately. which sucks.**

zoegirl: it's not her fault her parents gave her a cool
    name. I realize that. and it's not her fault that

	she, herself, is cool. I suppose it's also not her fault that stupid Oberlin has coed dorm halls AND coed bathrooms.
mad maddie:	**Oberlin has coed bathrooms?**
zoegirl:	Doug gets to see Canyon in her pj's! yay!
zoegirl:	Oberlin even has coed dorm rooms, but Doug at least didn't opt for that.
mad maddie:	**whoa**
mad maddie:	**if I went to Oberlin, I cld have a guy for a roommate?**
mad maddie:	**I don't know how I feel about that. I truly don't.**
zoegirl:	Canyon explained the philosophy behind it, not that I asked. she said the lack of "conventional boundaries" makes it so that guys and girls can be friends instead of seeing each other as sex objects, but what she MEANT was that Oberlin is just cooler than every other college in the world.
mad maddie:	**I'm still trying to wrap my head around the idea of having a dude for a roomie.**
mad maddie:	**I haven't met my own roomie, btw. I know what her name is—Zara—but for now I'm rooming with a girl named Shannon. she's cool.**
zoegirl:	why haven't you met your own roomie?
mad maddie:	**they mixed us up for orientation so that we meet more ppl. on Tuesday we move into our real dorm rooms. I'll meet Zara then.**
zoegirl:	oh
mad maddie:	**so, you went to Oberlin to see Doug. you met a girl named Canyon. at some point there was neediness, I'm assuming, and at some point Doug did/said something that made you sad/mad/ whatever . . . ?**
zoegirl:	BLAHHHHHHHH
zoegirl:	I drove all this way to see him, and when I got

	here, he was like, "Zoe. Awesome. It's so good to see you. So listen, I'm playing cards later with some ppl in my dorm. Wanna join?"
mad maddie:	"it's so good to see you"?!!
zoegirl:	"it's so good to see you" and "want to play cards?"
zoegirl:	that's weird, right?
mad maddie:	was Canyon one of the card-playing ppl?
zoegirl:	yes, and she and Doug shot "witty" remarks back and forth all night long.
mad maddie:	about what?
zoegirl:	about everything.
zoegirl:	politics, Oberlin's cafeteria food. some inside joke about "just the tip? just the tip?"
zoegirl:	it was hiLARious. Canyon thought so, anyway.
zoegirl:	also Canyon was wearing a tank top, and her bra strap kept slipping down, and she made sure everyone in the room knew all about it. every five minutes, she was like, "Omigod, my bra keeps falling off. Whoops, there it goes again!"
mad maddie:	at least she was wearing a bra. that's good, isn't it?
zoegirl:	no. yes. maybe. her bra was polka-dotted and adorable, and I hated it.
mad maddie:	some of the girls in my dorm are not perma-bra wearers. it is unnerving, not so much cuz of the lack of bra(s), but because I'm aware of the lack of bra(s). and because I'm aware of being aware.
mad maddie:	I mean, normally I'm the "pish-posh, who cares about conventions" girl, aren't I? isn't that *my* role?
zoegirl:	it is, yes. but not wearing a bra is . . . I don't know. I want to say tacky, but maybe I need to think about it.
zoegirl:	BUT ANYWAY, I finally pulled Doug away and said, "Don't you want to be with *me*?"

mad maddie:	ah, crap. and he wanted to keep playing cards with too-cool Canyon?
zoegirl:	😳
zoegirl:	I feel loserish in so many ways.
mad maddie:	Zoe. listen up, cuz this is important. do u and Doug have plans for the rest of the day?
zoegirl:	I don't know. He hasn't woken up yet. I'm hoping we'll go have breakfast together, just the two of us.
mad maddie:	stop hoping, cuz yr going to leave and yr going to leave NOW.
mad maddie:	do not pass go, do not collect $200. just grab yr stuff and tiptoe out of the room.
zoegirl:	???
zoegirl:	why?
mad maddie:	cuz he needs a taste of his own medicine. cuz he shld have treated you better, and he needs to be reminded of that.
zoegirl:	you really think I should just leave?
mad maddie:	hells yeah
zoegirl:	it wldn't be too rude?
mad maddie:	it wld be exactly the right amount of rude. go!

Sun, Sept 22, 7:30 PM E.D.T.

SnowAngel:	Madikins, I have been thinking.
mad maddie:	cool!
mad maddie:	I haz been eating the marshmallow moons out of my box of Lucky Charms. yolo!!!!
SnowAngel:	AHEM
SnowAngel:	I talked to Zoe this afternoon, and I can't get that girl Canyon out of my mind.
SnowAngel:	Canyon, who wore a cute polka-dot bra.
SnowAngel:	did Zo tell you about the cute polka-dot bra?
mad maddie:	she did, but I think Zoe was more concerned with the Canyon part than the bra part.

SnowAngel:	well, I know, silly. that's why I texted you instead.
mad maddie:	**me no understand**
SnowAngel:	you know the business class I'm in?
mad maddie:	**the one you registered for by accident?**
SnowAngel:	we have to come up with a fake start-up business. blah blah blah, boring boring kill me now.
SnowAngel:	we have to write a marketing plan and figure out overhead expenses and make a budget, and omg, it's going to be a TON of work.
mad maddie:	**is yr prof still a she-devil in sensible shoes?**
SnowAngel:	why does she think anyone cares about this stuff? who in their right mind wants to be an entrepreneur?
mad maddie:	**oh gee. I dunno. Bill Gates?**
SnowAngel:	who's Bill Gates?
mad maddie:	**exactly**
mad maddie:	**so what business are you going to start?**
SnowAngel:	none, obviously
SnowAngel:	but in Pretend Land, I'm thinking a store that sells really cute bras. isn't that brilliant?
mad maddie:	**like Victoria's Secret?** 😊
SnowAngel:	NO, cuz my store wld be better and cuter and adorabler. 🩲
mad maddie:	**you are nutso, A. I can't believe that Canyon's polka-dot bra is yr takeaway from Zoe's shitty night.**
SnowAngel:	does that make you not like me? 🙁
SnowAngel:	I *do* feel bad for Zo. but now I want a bra with polka-dot straps . . .
mad maddie:	**I think I will put lotion on my heels, which are a bit dry. come here, plz, lotion.**
SnowAngel:	and my business idea is good! I have deets and supporting evidence and everything, and the beautiful part is that I gathered it all just by living my life!

SnowAngel: so here's what I'm thinking. you know how you have to wear a nude-colored bra under a white t-shirt or cami?

mad maddie: ah, such soft feet. now to the elbows . . .

SnowAngel: I was BEMOANING that very fact last night when I put on my white cami as part of my kitty-cat costume.

SnowAngel: I was a white kitty cat, btw. everybody always goes as a black cat, have u noticed?

mad maddie: racist

SnowAngel: so . . . put it all together, and voila!

mad maddie: voila-wha?

SnowAngel: *drags whiteboard into middle of room* *whips out yummy-smelling whiteboard marker* *spells out genius idea*

SnowAngel: • cute bras are cute.

SnowAngel: • nude-colored bras are NOT cute.

SnowAngel: • nude-colored bra straps are especially uncute, especially when they peek out from under the straps of yr cami.

SnowAngel: are you with me?

mad maddie: in what way?

SnowAngel: and then I talked to Zo, and der! someone needs to make a nude-colored bra (the part that holds up yr boobies, or in my case, booblets) but with cute straps! stripes or polka dots or whatever!

SnowAngel: white cami? sure! and look! cute purple straps lining up all cutely with the white cami straps!

SnowAngel: but look closer. can you see the bra itself through the cute white cami? NO, YOU CANNOT, CUZ OF BRILLIANT SEKRIT NUDITY!

SnowAngel: 😀

SnowAngel: so whaddaya think???

mad maddie: I think they already exist. in fact, I know they do, cuz I have a bra that came with three sets of

	straps—all different colors—and you can switch them out whenever you want.
SnowAngel:	you do not
mad maddie:	**I do**
SnowAngel:	I completely reject that claim. how cld you possibly have a cute exchangeable bra-strap bra when I don't???
mad maddie:	**I think yr going to have to come up with a new business plan, love.**
SnowAngel:	no way, not unless my stupid business prof gets all uppity and says it's not BORING and BUSINESS-Y enough.
mad maddie:	**well, V's Secret works pretty damn well as a business.**
SnowAngel:	back to yr bra.
SnowAngel:	where did you buy it?
SnowAngel:	and can I have it?
SnowAngel:	I really think it shld belong to me since I thought of it first.
SnowAngel:	Maddie?
SnowAngel:	MADDIE!
SnowAngel:	ah, screw you. go have fun with yr effing lotion, ya loser!

Sun, Sept 22, 10:21 PM E.D.T.

zoegirl:	I saw your tweet. do you and your sorority sisters ever study?
zoegirl:	also, please tell me that you ALWAYS do that buddy thing at parties, where you watch after your friends and they watch after you. no going up to guys' rooms, no accepting drinks you didn't pour yourself or see poured, etc.
zoegirl:	you have to be careful. this isn't high school, you know.

zoegirl:	(although I kinda wish it was)
zoegirl:	(high school, I mean)
zoegirl:	(shhh)
zoegirl:	but yeah. so, anyway . . .
zoegirl:	I'm back from Oberlin. wasn't the best visit ever.
zoegirl:	sigh
zoegirl:	miss you, A.

Mon, Sept 23, 9:00 AM E.D.T.

SnowAngel:	yoo-hoo! Maddie! are you awake?
mad maddie:	**go away. sleeping.**
SnowAngel:	if yr sleeping, why'd you txt me back?
mad maddie:	**I said go away. I'm sleeping, fool.**
SnowAngel:	coochie-coochie-coo! *tickles Maddie's chin*
mad maddie:	**did you not hear me, woman? I am SLEEPING, so quit yer yammering!**
SnowAngel:	*folds hands in lap* *smiles pleasantly* *blinks*
SnowAngel:	you say you're sleeping, and yet . . .
SnowAngel:	you txted me back ONCE. then you txted me back TWICE. then you txted me back A THIRD TIME! ah ah ah! THREE messages from Maddie!
SnowAngel:	*roll of thunder*
SnowAngel:	*clap of lightning*
SnowAngel:	AH AH AH! 👿
SnowAngel:	that was me being the Count. 😀 😀 😀
SnowAngel:	you know, that vampire dude from "Sesame Street"?
SnowAngel:	*pokes Maddie*
SnowAngel:	u still there?
SnowAngel:	oh, Maddieeeeeeee!
mad maddie:	**OMG. my iPad flashes EVERY SINGLE TIME YOU MESSAGE ME! I'm putting you under my bed. g'night!**
SnowAngel:	but it's not night. it's morning. ☀
mad maddie:	**not in California**

SnowAngel: um, technically it is. I mean, it might be early, but . . .

SnowAngel: hey! this'll perk you up. I saw Ian last night. he looks GOOD, lady. (not in an I'm-after-your-man way, obvs, but just, he's a good man, your Ian.)

SnowAngel: confused, tho. he said you were feeling out of place??? except you're not, cuz you wld have told me if you were. right?

SnowAngel: M-babe?

SnowAngel: where you be, M-babe?

SnowAngel: omg, did you really put me under your bed?

SnowAngel: huh. at least there are snacks down here.

SnowAngel: 🥄🍼🍭

Mon, Sept 23, 9:14 AM P.D.T.

mad maddie: I'm awake. it is now nine o'clock here in California, ok? you texted at nine o'clock Georgia time, which was fricking SIX O'CLOCK Cali time. six in the morning is NOT Maddie time.

mad maddie: and as I am still fragile from having my sleep interrupted, I must request that you talk quietly. and with no exuberant hand movements.

SnowAngel: MADS! YAY! I was so happy when I saw you pop up on my laptop screen!

SnowAngel: I'm in geology now. soooooo boring, but the TA is handsome in a brooding Mediterranean sort of way.

mad maddie: ouch. just burned my tongue on my coffee.

SnowAngel: so wassup?

mad maddie: nothing, other than me, and my head hurts. anyway, *you* txted *me*. I'm just txting you back. messaging. whatever.

mad maddie: Angela?

mad maddie: you still there?

SnowAngel: sorry, sorry, back now. had to smile at TA while I non-answered a tricky question about . . . I dunno . . . rocks.

SnowAngel: what do you think's going to happen with Zo and Doug? do you think they're going to break up?

mad maddie: cuz of that Canyon girl? is that why you texted me?

SnowAngel: or maybe cuz of sex, cuz based on my observations (and ONLY observations, as I am the last virgin standing), college guys likie da sex.

SnowAngel: is it possible Doug's pulling away cuz of the sex thing?

mad maddie: what sex thing? the sex thing that involves him and Zoe having sex?

mad maddie: call me crazy, but I doubt Doug sees that as a problem.

SnowAngel: yeah, but that's *you* talking. you and Ian are really good at sex.

SnowAngel: oh! and what I asked earlier. ARE you feeling out of place at Santa Cruz???

mad maddie: no. maybe a little. but I only told Ian that cuz he said HE felt out of place sometimes, and I was being supportive.

SnowAngel: Ian feels out of place? here at UGA?

mad maddie: not as a general rule. just when his whole hall turns into a drunken redneck whooping party. times like that.

SnowAngel: awww, poor Ian. I hate thinking of him feeling like that.

SnowAngel: I think we all feel like that, tho. I bet every single person in college feels out of place at one time or another.

mad maddie: yeah. but.

mad maddie: that's the point of college: to go somewhere new, even if it pushes you out of your comfort zone. and, you know, to make it work. to be yourself anyway, only bigger and better and MORE.

SnowAngel: the next time I see Ian, I'll take time to hang out with him longer. friends need friends need friends! 💜

mad maddie: as far as sex goes, that makes me laugh that you think we're "better" at it than Zo and Doug.

SnowAngel: you're saying you're not?

mad maddie: no, I'm pretty sure we are. we weren't at first, tho. we had to practice for the whole summer. 😳

SnowAngel: Zoe and Doug have had more time to practice than that, and I don't get the impression that Zoe thinks it's a laugh a minute. or an orgasm a minute. 😊

mad maddie: dude. an orgasm a minute? you. would. die.

SnowAngel: that's why they call it seven minutes in heaven! HA! omg, I'm so brilliant.

SnowAngel: except, wait. wld seven orgasms send you to heaven? THAT heaven?

mad maddie: going out on a limb here, but I don't think two middle school kids + closet + seven minutes with friends outside listening and laughing = any orgasms at all.

SnowAngel: which brings us back . . .

SnowAngel: . . . to Zoe. you know it does. you *know* what I'm saying.

mad maddie: sighhhhhhhhhhhhhhhh

mad maddie: I do. but I also know that Zoe's working on it.

SnowAngel: "working on it"?

SnowAngel: shld sex be work?

mad maddie: sex shouldn't have "shoulds" and "shouldn'ts." this is something for Zo and Doug to figure out on their own.

SnowAngel: OH, PLEASE

SnowAngel: so yr not going to give them hands-on lessons?

mad maddie: I think someone's having unfulfilled libido issues. I think someone shld discuss this problem with handsome brooding TA!

Mon, Sept 23, 9:55 AM P.D.T.

mad maddie: Zoe. babe. orientation ends today, and tomorrow I meet my real roomie. I'm psyched, cuz I didn't really bond with the peeps in my orientation group. I mean, they were fine. there just wasn't enough time to develop Deep and Meaningful Relationships That Will Last Forever.

zoegirl: I'm supposed to be making Deep and Meaningful Relationships That Will Last Forever?

zoegirl: crap. I'm in trouble.

mad maddie: with my real roomie, it will be better. real roomie plus entire suite full of girls I'll be with for whole year. yay!

mad maddie: as for your crap, that is why I'm chatting you up, girl.

zoegirl: I can always tell when you're texting with your phone instead of your laptop or iPad because a) you're faster and b) you make fewer typos.

mad maddie: tipos? I never make tiptoes.

mad maddie: but I know. I'm faster with my thumbs. it's weird.

mad maddie: anywayz! back to your crap!

zoegirl: scatologist. 🍰

mad maddie: you just made that word up, college girl. I like it.

mad maddie: but if we cld stay on topic, plz . . . ?

mad maddie: I move my stuff to new dorm room tomorrow, and then on Wednesday classes start. time's a-tickin, things are happening! so I need yr answer, toots.

zoegirl: my answer to what?

mad maddie: such a coy mistress! I need you to sign the winsome threesome yolo pact for reals, and not just in theory like you said before.

zoegirl: omigosh, you're still thinking about that?

mad maddie: yes, cuz it's important. Angela and I are both in, but it won't count unless you are too.

mad maddie: *throws Zoe a Sharpie* *throws Zoe copy of pact written in fancy calligraphy writing*

mad maddie: now gimme yr John Adams

zoegirl: um . . . it's John Hancock

mad maddie: no, it's a purple Sharpie, cuz I know how you feel about purple. I'm showing you the love, yo!

zoegirl: you are a weirdo. but thank you, because it shows you know me. 🖤

zoegirl: no one here KNOWS me, Mads.

mad maddie: and that's why our pact matters. it'll make us get out there and do stuff, and when we get out there and do stuff, we'll get to know ppl—and they'll get to know us.

mad maddie: just promise already. sheesh. don't you want to make yer Auntie Maddie happy?

zoegirl: ok, fine.

mad maddie: that doesn't sound very enthusiastic.

zoegirl: ok, not fine.

mad maddie: whoa there! I'll take yr unenthusiastic fine! 👍

mad maddie: *kisses signed contract* *seals contract with wax and locks in fireproof safe*

mad maddie: thank you, hot stuff. now skedaddle. go forth and be awesome!

Tues, Sept 24, 2:02 PM E.D.T.

SnowAngel: your roomie! you must tell me! horns or no horns? 😈

mad maddie: I've known her for all of an hour, Angela. most of which has been spent unpacking and stuff.

SnowAngel: so? first impression, then. five words. go!

mad maddie: hmmm . . .

SnowAngel: doesn't count as a word. start over.

mad maddie: pretty

mad maddie: confident

mad maddie: from Santa Barbara

SnowAngel: LAME USE OF LAST THREE WORDS. Zara being from Santa Barbara tells me nothing.

mad maddie: um, beg to differ. it tells you she's from Santa Barbara, fool. also, it's kind of like you being from Atlanta and going to UGA.

SnowAngel: ???

mad maddie: she's local. ish. she's from California, not out of state like me. she already knows every girl in our suite.

SnowAngel: is that good or bad?

mad maddie: neither. it just is.

SnowAngel: well, do you like her?

mad maddie: sure. why not?

mad maddie: she's kinda loud, tho

SnowAngel: hahahaha! you, Maddie, are loud. for you to say that Zara's loud . . .

mad maddie: she has a tattoo on her arm of one of those little Japanese cats with its paw held up.

SnowAngel: cute or fugly?

mad maddie: it's cool.

SnowAngel: describe the rest of her, other than "pretty."

mad maddie: urrggh

mad maddie: cutoffs, tank top, tattoo. beaded bracelet wrapped many times around her wrist. toe ring. very friendly. but like I said, it's been all of an hour.

mad maddie: also, the door to our room is open. everyone's doors are open. is kind of a free-for-all. I'll tell you more once things have settled down!

mad maddie: ok, so that was Zara who came into the room just now—did you see her? I tried to subtly aim my laptop screen in her direction, but then I realized that if she glanced over, she'd totally be able to tell what I was doing. and then I accidentally hung up on you instead of just turning off visual. sorry!

zoegirl: no problem

mad maddie: and I switched to messaging cuz I don't want her first impression of me to be that I'm still glued to my high school besties.

mad maddie: I don't think I cld talk to you with her in the room, anyway. wld be too awkward.

zoegirl: I only saw the back of her. she's super tan.

mad maddie: yeah, everyone is. and I've now learned that ALL the girls in my suite went to the same high school, including Zara.

zoegirl: why isn't she rooming with one of the girls she knows?

mad maddie: cuz . . . she isn't? our suite is like an apartment. there's a kitchen, a bathroom, a hanging-out area, and four bedrooms, all of them doubles.

mad maddie: but there are seven girls in the Santa Barbara group. seven plus me equals eight, so they drew straws to see who'd get the newbie.

mad maddie: apparently Zara lost.

zoegirl: 😉

zoegirl: Zara *won*, you mean.

zoegirl: Zara didn't actually say that, did she? about drawing straws and being the one who lost?

mad maddie: nah, one of her other friends did, an uber-hip girl named Neesa.

mad maddie: Neesa's, like, the definition of California glam. skinny, gorgeous, mountain biker. earrings made out of beer cans. *that* girl—you know?

zoegirl: here at Kenyon, it's more like the Nerdy Girl Special. square-frame glasses, micro-bangs, retro Catholic schoolgirl skirts. they all have blogs with names like "Nerdy, Dirty, and Flirty."

zoegirl: should I start a blog?

mad maddie: no

zoegirl: ha

zoegirl: but I need to do SOMETHING to distract me from missing Doug.

zoegirl: do you miss Ian?

mad maddie: what do you think?

mad maddie: I try not to, but of course I do.

zoegirl: and I try not to miss Doug, but every day I epically fail.

zoegirl: actually, I *don't* try not to miss him. I'm not nearly as good at that stuff as you are.

mad maddie: what stuff?

zoegirl: making the best of things. deciding how something should be and then doing whatever it takes to make it happen.

mad maddie: I do that?

zoegirl: yes, and you know it.

zoegirl: like with college. you chose Santa Cruz because it was new and different and far away. you came up with the whole yolo pact as a way of saying, "It's up to us to make sure college is awesome, and so we will." I admire that so much about you!

mad maddie: hey, you said yes to the yolo pact too.

zoegirl: but it's easier for you.

zoegirl:	you're a force of nature! you're Maddie!
mad maddie:	**please**
zoegirl:	it's true.
zoegirl:	I, on the other hand, am just pathetic. everyone says college is supposed to be the time of our lives, but if that's true, I'm in BIG trouble.
mad maddie:	**oh, Zoe**
mad maddie:	**(((((((((((((HUGS)))))))))))))**
mad maddie:	**listen. forget about Doug for a minute and think about Kenyon. just plain Kenyon, without the awful missing-your-boyfriend factor. what are some things you like about Kenyon?**
zoegirl:	😐
mad maddie:	**oh, c'mon. there have to be *some* good things.**
zoegirl:	like what?
mad maddie:	**I don't know. the food? cuz I ♥ the Santa Cruz cafeterias with a mad passion. one swipe of my meal-plan card and I can have anything and everything I want.**
mad maddie:	**chicken alfredo? sure! chase it down with a cheeseburger and fries? why not?**
zoegirl:	you're making me feel ill. I would explode.
mad maddie:	**even the salad bar rocks, cuz there is a cheese section, which means I can heap shredded cheddar on everything and still feel healthy. NOM NOM NOM.**
zoegirl:	huh. do you put lettuce in these salads of yours?
mad maddie:	**now it's your turn. name something about college you like.**
zoegirl:	hmm . . .
zoegirl:	I like my creative writing class. I like all my classes, even though the workload is insane.
mad maddie:	**excellent start. keep going.**
zoegirl:	and everyone here is smart. I like that.

mad maddie: 👍

mad maddie: and . . . ?

zoegirl: well, I'm kind of in love with the campus. I should have thought of that before. it's so spread out and big and NOT high school. same with the town. I love walking around and exploring and discovering new places.

mad maddie: I like that part too. high school was fun, but there were a lot of walls.

zoegirl: yeah. and along those same lines, there are definitely things I like about living on my own. I like setting my own schedule and being in charge of my time and not having anyone nag me about homework.

mad maddie: see?

mad maddie: you've done some fine work here, Zo. keep it up!

Wed, Sept 25, 11:01 AM E.D.T.

zoegirl: really, Angela? REALLY???

SnowAngel: what?

zoegirl: your FB status. I do NOT approve!

SnowAngel: oh. that. well—as I said—I'm not thrilled about it either.

zoegirl: so don't do it! if I told you, "Oh, and by the way, this afternoon I'm going to put on my bikini and let frat boys draw all over my body," what would YOU say?

SnowAngel: it isn't my choice. I'm a pledge and we have to do whatever our sisters tell us to.

zoegirl: not that you have any "problem areas" in the first place. but I'm sure some of the girls do, at least in the opinion of the frat boys, and how are they going to feel if some guy draws a circle on their thigh or whatever and writes "TOO FAT"?

SnowAngel:	and I repeat: I don't want to do this either! IT'S NOT MY CHOICE.
zoegirl:	**Angela, this is hazing. isn't hazing against the law?**
SnowAngel:	I know it sounds messed up. it IS messed up. but my world is different from yours, all right?
zoegirl:	**how so?**
SnowAngel:	omg. cuz I'm in the most popular sorority at one of the biggest party schools in the South. I kinda signed up for this, Zoe, so cld you maybe be supportive instead of trying to make me feel bad?
zoegirl:	**but Angela . . .**
SnowAngel:	on the plus side, there might be Jell-O shots.
zoegirl:	**and that makes it better how . . . ?**
SnowAngel:	it's a bonding activity. that's all it is, and I'm not going to be the whiner baby who gets uptight about it.
SnowAngel:	Zo?
SnowAngel:	you still there?
zoegirl:	**I'm here. I just can't think of anything to say.**
SnowAngel:	well, thx for that confidence booster. what a pal.
	👍

Wed, Sept 25, 10:44 PM E.D.T.

SnowAngel:	Zoe keeps calling me, but I'm not in the mood to talk to her, so I'm not answering. yes, I'm mature that way.
SnowAngel:	how was yr first day of classes?
SnowAngel:	no, screw that. how was rock climbing with Zara and the Esbees?
mad maddie:	**the Esbees?**
SnowAngel:	the Santa Barbara girls.
mad maddie:	**???**
SnowAngel:	Santa Barbara.
SnowAngel:	S.B.
SnowAngel:	Esbees!

mad maddie: ahhh. clever.

SnowAngel: are they all that tan or did you use a filter on the pics you posted?

mad maddie: I'm so sore I can't walk. my knees are banged up, I tore off half a fingernail, and I didn't know how to put my harness on or tie any of the special knots. Zara had to help me, and she was nice about it, but toward the end I cld tell she was getting impatient.

SnowAngel: she's the one who invited you. she's not allowed to feel impatient.

mad maddie: yeah, cuz that's the way it works.

mad maddie: she and her buds have all these inside jokes, and most of their convos are about ppl I don't know. and they have these lewd nicknames for each other, like they call Neesa "Teesa" as in "cock teasa." and they were kind of crazy out there, racing up the cliff and then doing these victory yells from the top. I'm not saying that's BAD. it's just . . . I don't know.

mad maddie: but who cares, right? I went rock climbing! yay, me! 😊

SnowAngel: yay, you! you're such a stud!

SnowAngel: do you think Zo read my most recent FB status? the one that said how the bikini thing turned out to be a total joke?

mad maddie: did you go to a real frat house?

SnowAngel: ???

mad maddie: did you wear a real bikini?

SnowAngel: yes, but there were no Sharpies, no blindfolds, and no body-flaw identification rituals.

SnowAngel: we had to serve Jell-O shots off our bellies, THAT'S ALL IT TURNED OUT TO BE. and! for the record! tons of boys told me I looked hot in my bikini, and one guy said I had the best ass in the entire Zeta pledge class! 😜

mad maddie: um . . . that's a good thing?

SnowAngel: omg, crashing hard. g'night, sweet Mads, who unlike some ppl doesn't make me feel like a ho!

Thu, Sept 26, 8:44 AM P.D.T.

mad maddie: cheezus christ, I did **NOT** need to see that.

zoegirl: see what?

mad maddie: Zara.

mad maddie: squatting.

mad maddie: pulling down her underwear.

mad maddie: slapping on A PANTYLINER.

mad maddie: in our room! in front of me! "la la la, don't mind me, just putting on a pantyliner, la-di-da!"

zoegirl: EW. inappropriate!

mad maddie: agreed! 😖

mad maddie: but maybe I'm being a prude? maybe it's like the bra thing, and how some of the girls go around braless, and I don't want to notice, but I do?

zoegirl: I would not want to see anyone put on a pantyliner.

zoegirl: I definitely would not want anyone to see ME put on a pantyliner.

mad maddie: yes, and I'm right there with you. but I feel like I'm judging Zara, and I don't want to be a judging sort of person.

mad maddie: for what it's worth, she *did* offer me a pantyliner too.

zoegirl: please tell me you're kidding.

mad maddie: I'm kidding—altho, ha. that wld have been funny.

zoegirl: yeah, hilarious. that sounds like something YOU would do.

mad maddie: except minus the pantyliner part, which means I wldn't.

zoegirl: Maddie, I think you're judging yourself more harshly than you're judging Zara. and guess what? you are *totally* allowed to not want to see your roomie putting on a pantyliner.

mad maddie: yeah, yeah, yeah. but aren't I supposed to be the uninhibited one?

zoegirl: what do you mean?

mad maddie: I don't know. just that that's my job. I'm the wild one, Angela's the boy-crazy one, and you're the good-girl one.

zoegirl: the good-girl one? I don't want to be the good-girl one!

mad maddie: yes you do, cuz that's who you are. and I *thought* I was the wild one, only now Zara's flinging pantyliners around and telling me she's "yeasty" and screaming from the tops of mountains.

zoegirl: um, that was a lot of info all at once. head is spinning.

mad maddie: what makes it worse is that she clearly thinks I'm shy and is always apologizing for "freaking me out."

"zoegirl: I am very hesitant to ask, but . . . yeasty?

mad maddie: uh-huh. she shared that with me and the Esbees in the cafeteria line. said her groinal area was itching like a crackhead and asked Neesa if she would scratch it for her.

zoegirl: ew!

zoegirl: gross!

zoegirl: ick!!!

mad maddie: I know! that was my reaction! and then I started second-guessing myself, cuz if it had been ME who said that? if I said that to you and Angela, wld I have thought it was hysterical?

zoegirl: no thank you

mad maddie:	by Atlanta standards, I'm a badass, but in Atlanta, girls are taught to always be sweet and pretty and blah blah blah.
zoegirl:	meaning it's easier to be a badass in Atlanta?
mad maddie:	meaning—aaarrghhh.
mad maddie:	I. Chose. To come here.
mad maddie:	I chose to on purpose, with the specific goal of getting away from everything safe and familiar. I just need to chill out and give myself time to adjust.
zoegirl:	yes. and if anyone can do it, you can.
zoegirl:	plus you JUST got there. I have complete and utter faith in you, Mads. you're going to love Santa Cruz once you get used to it, I just know it.
mad maddie:	and with Zara . . . she is nice but, I mean, it's ironic. I moved three thousand miles away in order to get away from high school, and somehow I ended up smack-dab in the middle of a group of high school besties.
zoegirl:	😕
mad maddie:	but I'll get to know them better, Zara and the Esbees. it'll be fine.
mad maddie:	and now let's talk about you. are you still thinking about Doug 24/7 or are you getting out there and making friends?
zoegirl:	um . . . well . . .
mad maddie:	Zoe. that is not a good answer.
mad maddie:	what about the peeps in yr creative writing class? you like them, don't you?
zoegirl:	uh-huh
mad maddie:	so go up to one of them, stick out your hand, and say, "hello, my name is Zoe. wld you care to have a cup of coffee with me, new friend?"
zoegirl:	yeah, that'll happen

mad maddie: it will if you want it to.

mad maddie: let's make a deal: you find a way to hang out with the peeps from yr creative writing class, only OUTSIDE OF CLASS, and I'll keep trying with Zara and Neesa and those girls.

mad maddie: *fist thrust* yolo, baby! yeah!

zoegirl: I'm rolling my eyes at you . . . but I know you're right.

mad maddie: so it's a deal?

zoegirl: it's a deal.

zoegirl: at least neither of us has a Lucy to deal with, who has moved on from stealing Angela's Q-tips to, ahem, stealing the raisins out of her Raisin Bran.

mad maddie: and u say "ahem" because . . . ?

zoegirl: because who steals raisins out of Raisin Bran?!!! it is beyond nutso!

mad maddie: unless . . . maybe that's Lucy's way of getting closer to Angela? sniffing her Q-tips and savoring her raisins?

zoegirl: sniffing?

mad maddie: maybe that's what *you* shld do! Revised plan: go up to new friend, stick out hand, and say, "hello, my name is Zoe, and I am here to sniff your Q-tips." and follow up with "All Your Base Are Belong To Us!"

zoegirl: ???????????????

zoegirl: random random you are so random!!!!

mad maddie: Google it. that's my good girl.

mad maddie: I'll expect a full report by the end of the weekend!

Fri, Sept 27, 8:00 PM E.D.T.

SnowAngel: hey, lady. I'm getting ready for Zeta-Iota date party. it's called a "date party" cuz, unlike a mixer, you HAVE to show up with a date.

SnowAngel:	anyway, how do you like my hair? *preens* *fluffs*
mad maddie:	**Angela?**
SnowAngel:	yeah, babe?
mad maddie:	**I can't see yr hair.**
SnowAngel:	then answer my Skype, silly! why do you keep declining my call?
mad maddie:	**cuz I'm on quad and Zara is two feet away. I'd be self-conscious.**
SnowAngel:	you? self-conscious??? you've never been self-conscious in your life.
SnowAngel:	*I* think you're too busy being hip and swoo-swoo to answer my calls. *sniffs*
mad maddie:	**yeah, and that's why I'm texting you, which takes the exact same amount of time. FAULTY LOGIC, SISTER.**
mad maddie:	**I do feel self-conscious around Zara. seriously. but I'm going out with her tonight anyway, so there.**
mad maddie:	**what the hell is swoo-swoo?**
SnowAngel:	I am! I iz a sexy swoo-swoo bitch, that's what I iz! I found a Pinterest board on how to create casual beach waves using a straight iron, and I nailed it. I am a mermaid goddess! 🌊 🌊 🌊
mad maddie:	**when you say "I am a mermaid" . . .**
mad maddie:	**this isn't another one of those dress-up parties, is it?**
SnowAngel:	now, Maddie. does a date party sound to you like a "come as a mermaid" party?
mad maddie:	**yes? no? I know not the ways of you crazy sorority girls!**
SnowAngel:	you make me giggle, and no, I'm not dressing up as a mermaid, tho that's a good one to keep in mind for the car wash we're hosting tomorrow.
SnowAngel:	*taps chin* hrrm, where to find a good clamshell bra . . . ?

SnowAngel:	tonight I'm wearing skinny jeans and my vintage vest with tassels, which sounds horrid in concept but is, in reality, extremely awesome and makes my boobs look fantastico.
mad maddie:	**ah**
SnowAngel:	wanna know who my date is?
mad maddie:	**yes**
mad maddie:	**of course**
mad maddie:	**I am dying to know**
SnowAngel:	yr saying that in a robot voice, aren't u?
mad maddie:	**why no I am not whatever in the world wld make u think that hashtag liarpants hashtag starwarsdroid hashtag geeksrule**
SnowAngel:	*glares*
SnowAngel:	his name's Todd, he's hot, and he's an Iota, duh, since the Iotas are hosting the party.
mad maddie:	**oh, yeah, duh. absolutely.**
SnowAngel:	a Zeta named Beth set me up with him. she was like, "He talks about football too much, but he's a total catch. He's good in bed and he LOVES oral—and I'm not talking about you going down on him. I'm talking him going down on you."
mad maddie:	**wow**
mad maddie:	**that's, ah, a lot to take in. or—ha!—I guess it's NOT a lot to take in, if what that Beth girl says is true.**
SnowAngel:	heh?
SnowAngel:	oh. good lord, Maddie. u r just . . .
SnowAngel:	erggh! no taking in! not boy/girl OR girl/boy.
SnowAngel:	have u . . . er . . . taken in Ian?
mad maddie:	**why did the Beth girl pass Todd off on you if he's such a catch?**
SnowAngel:	is that a yes? taking that as a yes unless you say otherwise . . .
mad maddie:	**Angela, of course I've given Ian blow jobs. it's no**

	big deal, except that eventually yr jaw starts to hurt.
SnowAngel:	a tip to remember. gotcha.
mad maddie:	**well, der! the tip's the most sensitive part! licky like a lolly and give yr jaw a break!**
SnowAngel:	Oh. My. God. so gross.
SnowAngel:	I'm off to pre-party. a bunch of us are meeting in the kitchen for tequila shots so that when we get to the party we'll already have a buzz on. 🍸
mad maddie:	**once upon a time, *I* was the one who was considered the wild child. seems hard to believe now, doesn't it?**
SnowAngel:	😵 😵 😵
SnowAngel:	have fun with the Esbees!

Fri, Sept 27, 11:59 PM E.D.T.

SnowAngel:	ohhhh, Zooooeeeeee!
SnowAngel:	I am drunkie. 🍺 come play with meeeeeee!
zoegirl:	I would, but *I* am tucked snugly in my bed, reading "My Family and Other Animals." it's awesome.
SnowAngel:	is it about aniamals?
SnowAngel:	*animals
SnowAngel:	I like animals!
SnowAngel:	🐷 🐭 🐗 🐵 🐌 🐛 🐴 🐮
SnowAngel:	I'm a chicken! moooooooooo!
zoegirl:	it's about a kid who lives in Greece and all of his adventures. makes me want to go.
SnowAngel:	👍
zoegirl:	but earlier I made the bold move of going out to dinner WITH STRANGERS. well, not strangers, but a guy and a girl from my creative writing class. Holly and Gannon.
SnowAngel:	I did something with strangers too!!!!

SnowAngel:	well, ONE stranger.
SnowAngel:	my asshole date ditched me, so I got him back by kissing a verrrrrry cute boy named . . .
zoegirl:	. . . yes?
SnowAngel:	my goodness. it seems I do not know Cute Boy's name.
SnowAngel:	I knew it once. I am almost positive I did.
zoegirl:	why did your date ditch you?
SnowAngel:	Todd? who knows, who cares. buh-bye, Todd! hello, cute new boy!
zoegirl:	it's after midnight, Angela. I'm going back to bed.
SnowAngel:	because it's after midnight? what kind of reason is that?
SnowAngel:	I'm still at party. I'm going to celebrate this after-midnight business by finding Cute Boy again. more kissing! me like kissing!!!

Sat, Sept 28, 11:52 AM E.D.T.

zoegirl:	you awake?
zoegirl:	it's 9 o'clock in California land. it is NOT too early to be texting you.
zoegirl:	lame!!!

Sat, Sept 28, 10:05 AM P.D.T.

mad maddie:	u rang?
zoegirl:	I did! cuz I wanted to tell you that I did it: I went out with Holly and Gannon from my creative writing class, and it was so fun!
mad maddie:	my ladyfriend! way to go!
zoegirl:	we laughed and talked, and Holly ate a jalapeno pepper because she will try ANYTHING at least once (that's one of her mantras), and it was just . . . fun. and later I'm going to call Doug and have a good, normal conversation with him. I

feel like I can, now that I'm more me-ish. does
that make sense?

mad maddie: **what'd y'all do?**

zoegirl: we went to dinner at a place called the Zooming
Burrito.

zoegirl: our waiter started off being totally aloof, but
Holly is seriously the friendliest person I have
EVER met, and she kept trying to draw him out.
she said her theory is that most people who come
across as rude are actually shy, but that everyone
needs human interaction, so she doesn't let their
rudeness put her off. she just tries harder.

mad maddie: **huh. cld be awesome, cld be insanely annoying.**

zoegirl: eventually she said flat out, "So, Teddy, what's
your story?"

mad maddie: **Teddy = waiter?**

zoegirl: Teddy equals waiter.

zoegirl: Holly propped her chin on her hands and looked
up at him, smiling and waiting, and finally he told
us that he'd just moved to Ohio from Wyoming,
and that everything was still new to him, and that
he wanted to be a chef one day . . .

zoegirl: he basically went on and on, and it was cool. it
was obvious that he was happy to have someone
take an interest in him, you know?

mad maddie: **Holly sounds like Angela**

zoegirl: yeah, kinda, but Holly is more . . .

zoegirl: hmm. Angela is a people person for sure. but
Holly takes it a step further. she, like, loves the
whole world and not just people. she says she
wants to experience every single thing she can.
ooo—she's like YOU in that way!

mad maddie: **hahahaha**

zoegirl: and speaking of, how is your end of the deal going?

mad maddie:	pretty well.
zoegirl:	spill
mad maddie:	um, I went out with Zara and the Esbees. I had a fun time too.
zoegirl:	did you really, or are you just saying that?
mad maddie:	how lame wld that be, to lie about my evening's fun-ness? gee, thx, Zo.
zoegirl:	forgive me. details, please.
mad maddie:	well . . . you sure you can handle it?
zoegirl:	I'm pretty sure I can
zoegirl:	yes?
mad maddie:	we went to a casino and played blackjack. it rocked.
zoegirl:	whoa. for reals?
mad maddie:	AND—pregnant pause—it turns out that yrs truly is a whiz at counting cards. (and apparently no one can read my puh-puh-puh-puh-puh-poker face.)
zoegirl:	Maddie! double whoa!
zoegirl:	but don't you have to be 21 to gamble?
mad maddie:	ah, technically. it didn't seem to be a problem.
zoegirl:	did they check IDs? was there a bouncer or something?
mad maddie:	do you want me to be retroactively busted? fine, I'll go turn myself in.
zoegirl:	no—sorry sorry sorry. you're getting your Maddie-ness back, just like I'm getting my Zoe-ness back. forgive my Good Girl nail-biting?
mad maddie:	sure, kid. *ruffles Zoe's hair*
mad maddie:	anywayz, I walked away a hundred bucks richer, while Zara came out sixty dollars short, not that I'm gloating.
mad maddie:	well, maybe I am. but Zo?
zoegirl:	yeah?
mad maddie:	we did it, sweet cheeks. we rock!

SnowAngel:	ow. ow. ow-ow-ow.
SnowAngel:	it hurts to even type! don't you care?
zoegirl:	**you haven't given me time to care!**
zoegirl:	**what's wrong? do you have a hangover?**
SnowAngel:	no!
SnowAngel:	yes. 😞
SnowAngel:	but that's not why I'm in the HOSPITAL.
zoegirl:	**you're in the hospital?**
zoegirl:	**omigosh, why? are you ok? what happened???**
SnowAngel:	*lifts chin and looks proudly into distance* yeah, sure, *now* yr all concerned.
zoegirl:	**"proudly"?**
SnowAngel:	yeah, as soon as I hit "send," I realized that didn't sound right.
SnowAngel:	not proud as in, "ooo, I got an A!"
SnowAngel:	proud like Scarlett O'Hara when she vows never again to wear curtains or eat carrots. you know. she presses the back of her hand to her forehead and gazes off bravely, and her hair is windblown, and she's like, "no, no, don't feel sorry for me! I can take care of myself!"
zoegirl:	**Scarlett O'Hara never vowed to stop eating carrots, sweetie.**
zoegirl:	**are you really in the hospital???**
SnowAngel:	trivia question: do you know what the tongue of a belt is? trivia answer: it's the sticky-uppy part of the buckle, the metal prong-thing that you poke thru the belt hole.
SnowAngel:	only instead of sticking thru the hole in my belt, the tongue in question is sticking thru. my. foot.
SnowAngel:	my foot! waaaaaaaaaaaaah! and it's STILL THERE!
zoegirl:	**crap, are you kidding me?**
SnowAngel:	I'm not, and it's sticking ALL THE WAY thru my foot,

and I cld touch the end of it if I wanted to. believe
me, I don't.

zoegirl: I'm confused. snap me a pic.

SnowAngel: but . . . but . . . that means sitting up, which means
moving . . .

SnowAngel: owwieeeee!!!

SnowAngel: ok, hold on . . .

zoegirl: omfg! Angela! you have a BELT stuck in yr foot!

SnowAngel: told ya

zoegirl: would you please EXPLAIN?

zoegirl: holy frick, that looks so insanely painful.

SnowAngel: it is. now I know how Jesus felt.

zoegirl: and you're texting me while it's still in there? just
calmly texting away?

SnowAngel: not supposed to use cells in ER, so can't call.

SnowAngel: and I'm at hospital AND on drugs, per yr question
above. 💊

SnowAngel: don't misunderstand. I am still barely holding on to
the strings of life and will require much pampering
for days on end. but how cld I not txt my Zoe?

zoegirl: sheesh, Angela. my foot is hurting for you. and
also, normal ppl do not end up with belts stuck
through their feet.

zoegirl: how did this happen?

SnowAngel: well, last night was the date party, remember?

zoegirl: your date ditched you and you kissed a random
guy whose name you don't know. yes, I
remember.

SnowAngel: I kissed a random guy? really?

zoegirl: omg. go back and read your texts from last night.

SnowAngel: huh. intriguing.

SnowAngel: well, I do have this hazy impression that I drank kind
of a lot, so I crashed as soon as I got back to my
dorm room.

zoegirl:	so you got drunk. you went straight to bed. and???
SnowAngel:	whoazy there. never said *straight* to bed. I got undressed first (I do that sometimes 😊), only I was so wiped that I left my jeans and shirt on the floor.
SnowAngel:	and then in the middle of the night I had to pee, so I stumbled out of bed, only it was dark . . .
SnowAngel:	so yeah, I stepped on the clump of clothes, and I guess the tongue of my belt was sticking straight up, cuz it went clean thru my foot.
zoegirl:	OW! ow ow ow!
SnowAngel:	the RA on my hall called an 🚑 . it was exciting.
zoegirl:	and again, here you are texting merrily away with a belt dangling from your foot.
SnowAngel:	Vicodin is my new best friend.
zoegirl:	why haven't they taken it out yet? why haven't YOU taken it out yet? can't you just give it a good hard yank?
SnowAngel:	apparently my foot muscles have tightened up around the tongue, so no.
SnowAngel:	not *my* tongue. that wld be weird. the belt's tongue.
zoegirl:	riiiiight. which isn't weird at all.
SnowAngel:	they're going to shoot a muscle relaxant straight into my tootsie to make my muscles relax, but first they had to call my parents or something. plus there was a kid in front of me with RAT-BITE FEVER. *shudders*
SnowAngel:	but maybe it's finally my turn, cuz a guy in scrubs is heading my way. mwah!

Mon, Sept 30, 3:30 PM P.D.T.

mad maddie: I just spent the last TWO HOURS Skyping with Angela. am I such a good friend or what?

zoegirl:	is she still loopy?
mad maddie:	**ohhhhh yeah. she kept making her crutches talk to me. as far as puppet shows go, it left much to be desired.**
zoegirl:	she is so funny about those crutches. she's so proud of them! how many selfies did she post on Instagram of her and her crutches? twenty? thirty?
mad maddie:	**dude, she has a hole in her foot. I think she's earned the privilege.**
zoegirl:	yes. true. oh, and I sent her some chocolates from both of us, just so you're in the loop.
mad maddie:	**excellent idea. thx.** 👍
zoegirl:	hey, I'm meeting Holly and Gannon in half an hour, or maybe just Holly if Gannon hasn't gotten far enough on his history paper. (omg, workload here is crazy!)
zoegirl:	and guess what else? yesterday I went to the student center with the two of them and watched a Japanese movie called "My Neighbor Totoro," which made me cry.
mad maddie:	**aw**
zoegirl:	Holly's good about finding off-the-beaten-track sorts of things to do. it's cool.
zoegirl:	I feel so much better about myself, and just plain happier, now that I'm getting out and doing stuff—so thanks for making me.
zoegirl:	what about you? do you have plans?
mad maddie:	**um, it's Monday, the most boring day of the week. do I need plans?**
zoegirl:	I read yr tweet about how you haven't left your room except to go to class, that's all.
mad maddie:	**ahhh, yr worried I'm a big fat loser. gotcha.**
zoegirl:	ha ha

zoegirl:	I'm just hoping things are still going well with Zara and the Esbees, cuz I also read your earlier tweet, which was funny but also sad.
zoegirl:	who said you looked like death?
mad maddie:	**Neesa, but I'm sure she meant it in a kind way. plus, I tweet for effect, you know that.**
zoegirl:	"You look like death, but I mean it in a kind way"???
mad maddie:	**humor! it is called humor! and she was right. I did. it happens, ok?**
mad maddie:	**however, altho I *was* in my dorm room for most of the day, I am now sitting in the parking lot of Roller Land, looking Very Stylish in shorts and knee-highs. my hair is even in pigtails, and I've gotta go, chickie. time to clock in for the roller derby jam I signed up for.**
zoegirl:	roller derby jam?
mad maddie:	**Zara begged me to. they needed a fifth skater cuz Taylor—one of the Esbees—wimped out.**
zoegirl:	you, on a roller derby team. omg, that is so perfect. you will ROCK it, Mads.
mad maddie:	**course I will. it's all about grabbing life by the horns, right? I am a girl of my word.**
zoegirl:	you are my hero. I am in awe.
zoegirl:	what's the right way to say good luck to someone before a roller derby? it can't be "break a leg" . . .
mad maddie:	**how about "knock 'em dead, tiger!"**
zoegirl:	knock 'em dead, tiger!

Tues, Oct 1, 5:43 PM E.D.T.

SnowAngel:	Zoe! shhhh! *holds finger to lips*
SnowAngel:	(whisper voice) there's a dumpster behind our dorm, and guess who I just saw walking mysteriously toward it and then mysteriously away from it?

zoegirl:	I don't know! (why are we whispering?)
SnowAngel:	so that nobody hears us, silly!
SnowAngel:	IT WAS LUCY. my roommate was mysteriously lurking around the dumpster, and I must know why!
zoegirl:	maybe she was throwing away trash?
SnowAngel:	*snorts*
SnowAngel:	that's cute, Zo, but I saw no trash bag swinging casually from her hand.
SnowAngel:	also she was whistling a merry little tune. who whistles merry little tunes when she takes out her trash?
zoegirl:	how do you know she was whistling a merry little—
zoegirl:	wait a sec. Angela? if you were close enough to hear Lucy's merry little tune . . . are *you* lurking around the dumpster?
SnowAngel:	no, I'm watching from my dorm room window.
zoegirl:	then why are we whispering? ARE we still whispering?
zoegirl:	and how could you have heard Lucy's merry little tune from your dorm room window?
SnowAngel:	maybe I have extraordinary powers of hearing. did you think of that?
SnowAngel:	her mouth was pursed in an "O" shape and she was, like, nodding her head in a merry tune sort of way.
zoegirl:	wait a second. you are NOT in your dorm room, you liar! three minutes ago you updated your FB status to "soaking in the warm fall sun." you just want me to think you're in your dorm room so I don't yell at you for not taking care of your broken foot!
SnowAngel:	perforated, not broken. and I'm using my crutches, so I am so taking care of my foot.

zoegirl:	you're only supposed to use your crutches when you have to. otherwise you're supposed to rest!
SnowAngel:	I'll rest when I die.
SnowAngel:	anyway, I like my crutches. they make ppl do things for me. and I'm not in my dorm room. fine. but I'm sitting down, which means I'm not standing on my perforated foot, so hush.
zoegirl:	wait. huh? where are you then? are you behind the dumpster too?
SnowAngel:	dude, you're complicating things unnecessarily.
zoegirl:	*I* am? *I'm* complicating things unnecessarily???
SnowAngel:	I was coming back from a meeting with my biz prof. as suspected, she didn't like my first business plan proposal, so she made me come up with a better idea. one that has to do with utility instead of goods.
SnowAngel:	do you know what that means?
zoegirl:	no. do you?
SnowAngel:	it means I shld capitalize on my capacity to be useful to others. it means I'll be providing a service instead of a product, which is lucky, since cute bra straps are easy to talk about but hard to make.
zoegirl:	you sound so smart, Angela. I love it.
zoegirl:	does this mean you're actually liking your business class now?
SnowAngel:	let's not go that far.
SnowAngel:	let's just say it's kinda sorta *maybe* more interesting than I first thought.
SnowAngel:	and I don't hate my prof quite so much anymore either. not that I ever HATED her, but let's just say her sensible shoes no longer bother me as much as they shld.
zoegirl:	gasp!

SnowAngel:	I know, right? anyway, she says I have ingenuity, which is crucial if you want to be an entrepreneur. it made me feel good.
zoegirl:	awww
SnowAngel:	so. was hobbling from prof's office back to my dorm room, and that's when I spotted Lucy. as I am a curious sort, I hid in a sunny spot by the dumpster to see what she was up to.
SnowAngel:	she's gone now, but I'm happy here, so . . . *shrugs*
SnowAngel:	also I'm hiding from my sorority sisters until dinner is over.
zoegirl:	why?
SnowAngel:	cuz the pledges aren't allowed to eat anything but white bread and American cheese sandwiches for an entire week. I'm only one day in, and . . . yeah. not working for me. 👎
zoegirl:	is this another hazing-that-isn't-hazing ritual?
SnowAngel:	I assumed it wld turn out to be fake, just like the bikini/Jell-O shot night. I assumed that when we showed up at the Zeta house this morning, there'd be a fabulous breakfast buffet waiting for us. 🍩 🔍 🍫 🥐 ☕
zoegirl:	but no?
SnowAngel:	but no. just packs of cellophane-wrapped sandwiches. each pledge gets six a day: two for breakfast, two for lunch, two for dinner.
zoegirl:	disgusting
SnowAngel:	yeah, so I ordered chicken fingers, fried dill pickles, and a steak from the Blind Pig Tavern. plus peanut butter pie. plus a 32 oz Diet Coke.
SnowAngel:	they don't normally deliver, but I sweet-talked the guy who took my order into making an exception.

zoegirl:	where is he going to deliver it TO? the sunny spot behind the dumpster?
SnowAngel:	NEAR the dumpster, and yeah. I said to look for the girl in the sparkly tank top with crutches.
zoegirl:	two things: 1) drop out of your sorority, and 2) I'm glad you ordered some real food, but you need to eat a fruit or vegetable!
SnowAngel:	yr so funny. a pickle IS a vegetable, silly!

Tues, Oct 1, 6:17 PM E.D.T.

SnowAngel:	oh, there's something else I wanted to tell u!
SnowAngel:	actually two things.
SnowAngel:	u there?
SnowAngel:	well, fine.
SnowAngel:	thing one: I saw Ian on the quad and we talked about Maddie. only apparently she didn't tell him about her casino night OR her roller derby night. he had NO CLUE about either.
SnowAngel:	he started to seem a little sad that I knew stuff about her that he didn't.
SnowAngel:	I guess she didn't want him to feel bad that she was having all these crazy adventures without him. Like she wasn't missing him.
SnowAngel:	I got worried that I'd accidentally busted her, but I covered it pretty well. I blamed it on the Vicodin, and then I told him that YOU were taking skydiving lessons—ha ha ha, like that wld ever happen— and he looked at me like I was crazy and asked if I needed him to walk me to my dorm room or anything.
SnowAngel:	also he said that Maddie sucks at cards.
SnowAngel:	and now thing two: turns out the random boy I kissed at the date party is the boyfriend of a Zeta named Mae.

| SnowAngel: | apparently Mae's mad at me, so that's another reason not to swing by the Zeta house. |
| SnowAngel: | but I didn't know who he was when I kissed him! AND I STILL DON'T! |

Tues, Oct 1, 6:20 PM E.D.T.

SnowAngel:	one last thing.
SnowAngel:	saw the pic you posted of you and Holly. y'all look palsy-walsy!!!! you have yr arms around each other and everything!
SnowAngel:	(she has BIG bazoombas. wowza. I wish I had big bazoombas.)
SnowAngel:	k, bye for real. mwah!

Wed, Oct 2, 7:00 PM E.D.T.

zoegirl:	I'm at library but can't concentrate. can you chat, or are you busy?
mad maddie:	**I am completely chattable. wassup?**
zoegirl:	it's longish. you're sure you're not off to do something exciting with Zara and the Esbees?
mad maddie:	**I was gonna go surfing with them, but there's a shark alert, so that got scratched.**
zoegirl:	you surf now?
zoegirl:	Maddie, you are so full of it.
mad maddie:	**Zo. I live in a beach town. ppl surf here.**
mad maddie:	**I haven't actually gone surfing YET, but Zara was going to teach me. we just had to put it off.**
zoegirl:	but what if it turns out like the rock climbing thing and you end up not having fun?
mad maddie:	**who said I didn't have fun rock climbing?**
mad maddie:	**you're being strange, Zoe. are you stalling???**
zoegirl:	about what?
mad maddie:	**about whatever you txted about . . .** 😕
zoegirl:	ARGH.

zoegirl:	it's so dumb—or maybe it isn't. but earlier tonight I called Doug, and guess who answered? Canyon! that girl from his hall!
mad maddie:	**she had Doug's phone? why?**
zoegirl:	she was in his room studying. that's what she said.
zoegirl:	she said Doug had gone on a food run, but that he forgot his phone, and when she saw it was me who was calling, she decided to answer.
mad maddie:	**WHY?**
zoegirl:	because she "likes" me, apparently. she thinks I'm "great."
zoegirl:	she was around me for a few hours that night I visited Doug. she was witty and cute, and, if I'm being honest, she was totally nice to me. if we had met in any other way, I probably would've liked her too.
zoegirl:	but none of that matters, because one girl shouldn't answer another girl's boyfriend's phone. right?!!
mad maddie:	**do you think something's going on with the two of them?**
zoegirl:	I don't know! but my heart is racing and I feel like throwing up and I seriously might faint.
mad maddie:	**all right, well, first you need to take some deep breaths. you're going to be ok, you're not going to faint, you're not going to throw up.**
zoegirl:	I might
zoegirl:	do *you* think something could be going on? do you think Doug would ever cheat on me?
mad maddie:	**give me a second. I'm trying to imagine how I'd feel if I called Ian and this happened . . .**
zoegirl:	ACK. nauseated. putting head between knees.
mad maddie:	**ok, listen. ppl forget their phones all the time.**

	I can easily see Ian going on a food run and leaving his phone behind.
zoegirl:	but what if you called and a random girl answered?
zoegirl:	only not random. a girl who lives on Ian's hall and plays cards with Ian and shares a BATHROOM with Ian. a girl you know Ian likes, *supposedly* just as a friend, but who knows?????
mad maddie:	**I wldn't like it, but I wldn't want to overreact either. not without knowing more.**
zoegirl:	so you think I'm overreacting?
mad maddie:	**I'd want to hear what Ian had to say before jumping to conclusions, that's all. did Doug think it was weird that Canyon answered his phone?**
zoegirl:	I don't know. he hasn't called me back. but Maddie, I haven't told you the worst part.
mad maddie:	**uh-oh**
zoegirl:	Canyon didn't just say, "oh, Doug's not here, but I'll tell him you called." instead she dropped her voice and took on this concerned tone and told me she thinks Doug just wants to be *single* for a while.
mad maddie:	**whoa. wtf???**
mad maddie:	**what did you say back?**
mad maddie:	**no. rewind. start at the beginning and tell me the whole convo.**
zoegirl:	sighhhhhhh
zoegirl:	I called Doug. Canyon answered. she said, "Zoe! Hi! This is Canyon!"
mad maddie:	**SO strange**
zoegirl:	she told me Doug was on a food run, and I was like, "oh" or whatever, but on the inside I was blank because I was trying to figure out WHY SHE'D ANSWERED MY BOYFRIEND'S PHONE.

zoegirl:	she obviously didn't think it was strange at all, though, because she kept talking, asking me how my classes were and if it was starting to get cold in Gambier yet, stuff like that.
mad maddie:	**she asked about the weather? seriously?**
zoegirl:	when Oberlin is practically right next to Kenyon! I KNOW!
zoegirl:	so blah blah blah, I answered her questions, but as soon as there was a pause, I was like, "so Doug's getting food? how come? are you guys studying or something?"
zoegirl:	and she said, "yeah, but not just me and Doug—a whole group of us."
mad maddie:	**good! that means it wasn't just the two of them.**
zoegirl:	except she said that part really quickly, and I didn't hear ANY other voices in the background.
zoegirl:	then there was this long pause, and I could hear her breathing, and it was soooo awkward. but right when I was about to get off, she said, "can I tell you something that you probably don't want to hear, but maybe you do?"
mad maddie:	**exsqueeze me? no, she can't, and why wld she put it like that?**
mad maddie:	**it's like when someone starts a sentence with "no offense, but . . ."**
zoegirl:	that's when she turned on her sympathetic voice. she said, "you know Doug loves you, right? I mean, like, so much."
mad maddie:	**ugh ugh UGH**
mad maddie:	**she feels qualified to tell you this *why*?**
zoegirl:	"but he's struggling," she said.
zoegirl:	I asked what she meant, and she said, "it's complicated, because college is the only time

	in life when you can date anyone you want, you know?"
mad maddie:	what the hell? college isn't the only time in life when you can date anyone you want. ANY time in life is when you can date anyone you want.
zoegirl:	she said it was "awesome" how much Doug and I cared about each other, but that even so, the best thing I could do was give him some space.
mad maddie:	???
mad maddie:	I hate this chick! and Zoe, I am so sorry. AND pissed. do you have her number? do you want me to call her?
zoegirl:	I asked her if Doug said those very words, that he wanted space, and she hesitated and said, really softly, "pretty much, yeah."
mad maddie:	omg! she is so full of it! she's trying to mess with your head, I swear.
zoegirl:	is she?
zoegirl:	would she make up an entire conversation like that?
mad maddie:	she might
zoegirl:	I don't know. sounded too detailed to be completely untrue. but even if she made up any of it, why were she and Doug talking about our relationship in the first place?
mad maddie:	YOU DON'T KNOW THAT THEY WERE! she's pretending to know more about him than she really does to freak you out. she *wants* you to think something's up b/w them.
mad maddie:	and to answer your question from earlier? if some girl said all that to me about Ian, then yes, I wld be worried, and yes, I wld think something was wrong.

zoegirl:	I feel sick.
mad maddie:	thing is, you don't know how wrong the wrong thing is, or even WHAT the wrong thing is, and the only person who does is Doug.
mad maddie:	you need to call him, Zoe
zoegirl:	I'm scared
mad maddie:	I know—and the whole thing SUCKS. I wish I weren't so far away from you!
zoegirl:	I do too
mad maddie:	but there's something you need to remember, which is that Canyon has known Doug for what, a month? you've known him forever. AND HE IS DOUG. he's a good guy.
mad maddie:	plus, der, you know waaaaaay more about what's going on b/w the two of you than she ever will. call him, Zoe, ok?
zoegirl:	I know, you're right . . .
mad maddie:	cuz I am. I always am. call da boy!

Wed, Oct 2, 7:45 PM E.D.T.

zoegirl:	I did something bad, Angela.
zoegirl:	I was planning to tell Maddie the bad thing—she and I were just texting, and I fully intended to tell her the whole story—but I chickened out and told her only part of it.
SnowAngel:	ooo, then tell me!
SnowAngel:	I am in a borrrrrrrring Zeta chapter meeting and it is soooooooo borrrrrring, so entertain me with yr badness!
zoegirl:	it isn't "entertaining." it makes me sad that you think my problems are "entertaining."
SnowAngel:	I don't. I'm sorry. I'm just bored, but I'm not anymore.
SnowAngel:	what's the dealio?

zoegirl:	things are weird—again—with Doug, only I think it's more that things are STILL weird. as in, things never un-weirded since I saw him the weekend before last.
SnowAngel:	meaning what?
zoegirl:	the last time we had sex? when I drove up to Oberlin? it was bad.
SnowAngel:	bad how?
zoegirl:	it's embarrassing and pathetic. I've been wanting to tell you, but I haven't. and Maddie doesn't know either.
SnowAngel:	omg, so many secrets. Maddie's keeping stuff from Ian, you're keeping stuff from Maddie . . .
SnowAngel:	whatever this new thing is, just tell me, and I will listen and hold your hand and be supportive. I'm not in my silly mood anymore, I promise.
zoegirl:	you already know that the visit wasn't, like, a romantic getaway.
SnowAngel:	cuz he was being a card-playing dwerp. yah.
zoegirl:	but I assumed things would get more romantic once it was just the two of us.
zoegirl:	I assumed we'd have sex that night, if nothing else!
SnowAngel:	does sex = romance?
zoegirl:	well . . . it's supposed to. isn't it?
zoegirl:	but we didn't, cuz Doug's roommate was there.
SnowAngel:	Doug didn't tell him to leave?
zoegirl:	yeah, that was my thought. why didn't Doug ever tell him to leave???
zoegirl:	then on Sunday morning I woke up before Doug. I was depressed and blah cuz of how the visit had gone so far, so I texted Maddie, and she told me I should leave without saying good-bye.
SnowAngel:	to punish Doug. I remember.

zoegirl:	so I said, "you're right, you're right, I will."
SnowAngel:	ohhhh. but if you're telling me this . . .
SnowAngel:	I take it you didn't leave w/o saying good-bye after all?
zoegirl:	not exactly
zoegirl:	I kind of stayed in his bed until he woke up, and we snuggled, and for a while we watched some stupid NASCAR show with his roommate.
SnowAngel:	they have a TV in their dorm room?
zoegirl:	it's his roommate's. it's wall-mounted. Oberlin kids are RICH.
SnowAngel:	huh. I'm happy with my tablet, thx very much
SnowAngel:	but is that the badness? that instead of blowing him off, you stayed and watched cars zooming around a track?
zoegirl:	no. gets worse.
zoegirl:	after a while his roommate got up and went to the dining hall, meaning Doug and I were finally alone. so I lay there thinking, "um, ok, aren't you going to take advantage of this?"
zoegirl:	but he didn't. so I did.
SnowAngel:	naughty Zoe! I don't think that's bad. I think it's GREAT!
zoegirl:	well, don't.
zoegirl:	I climbed on top of him and started kissing him in a way that said very clearly, "here I am, ready to have sex! don't you want to?"
SnowAngel:	did YOU want to?
zoegirl:	kind of. I don't know. as much as I ever do?
zoegirl:	I definitely wanted him to, though.
zoegirl:	meaning I wanted *him* to want to. I wanted him to want *me*, to prove that everything was still good between us.
SnowAngel:	and?

zoegirl: eventually he got into it too, and it was all good— or so I thought.

zoegirl: but then . . .

SnowAngel: oh no. what happened?

zoegirl: I was still on top, and he was . . . AGH.

zoegirl: he was, um. he had his mouth on my . . .

zoegirl: he was kissing, or actually more like sucking, my . . .

zoegirl: do I have to say it? aren't you going to jump in?

SnowAngel: he was enjoying yr beautiful boobies?

zoegirl: that's not the way I would have put it, but yeah.

SnowAngel: what's wrong with that? yay for enjoying your beautiful boobies!

zoegirl: except I pulled back a little, so I could gaze into his eyes, AND HE WAS WATCHING TV!

zoegirl: we were having sex, and he was INSIDE me, and he was doing what you said to my boobs . . . and the whole time he was looking over my shoulder and watching that dumb car show!

SnowAngel: he cld see the tv with yr boob in his mouth?

zoegirl: ANGELA!

SnowAngel: I'm just trying to imagine this. I'm trying to make sure I have the full picture.

zoegirl: he could see the tv, yes. it was extremely obvious.

SnowAngel: un. cool.

SnowAngel: what did you say?

zoegirl: nothing

SnowAngel: wait. what?

SnowAngel: you kept having sex?!

zoegirl: I pretended not to notice. I told you I was pathetic.

SnowAngel: oh, sweetie

SnowAngel: (((((((((HUGS)))))))))

zoegirl: and things have been weird ever since then, and

	they just keep getting weirder. I keep thinking, "we just need to have a good long talk and things will get better," but we keep NOT having good long talks.
zoegirl:	I feel like I haven't talked to him in forever, not in a real way, and it's all just . . .
zoegirl:	it's just so . . .
SnowAngel:	fucked up?
zoegirl:	*nods*
SnowAngel:	ah, Zo. I'm so sorry.
SnowAngel:	is there anything I can do to make you feel better?
zoegirl:	tell me you love me anyway, even though I'm so fucked up?
SnowAngel:	you're not f'd up! the situation is!
SnowAngel:	YOU ARE WONDERFUL AND DOUG IS A DINGUS!!!
zoegirl:	hmmm
SnowAngel:	you believe me, right?
SnowAngel:	and of course I love you. I will always love you.
zoegirl:	
zoegirl:	I'll always love you too.

Wed, Oct 2, 8:31 PM E.D.T.

SnowAngel:	me again. I keep feeling sad for you!
SnowAngel:	wld it make u feel better to know that I have a hole in my foot? and am hobbling about piteously (but heroically) on crutches?
zoegirl:	I already know both of those things.
SnowAngel:	oh
SnowAngel:	wld it make u feel better to know that sure, you might have had bad sex, but I've never had sex at all?
zoegirl:	no
SnowAngel:	damn. two strikes.
SnowAngel:	um, wld it make u feel better to know that not only

am I STILL EATING DODGY CHEESE SANDWICHES FOR
EVERY MEAL, but that half the Zetas shoot me dirty
looks every chance they get?

SnowAngel: because of Mae, whose boyfriend I supposedly
kissed.

SnowAngel: does that make u feel even a little better?

zoegirl: **why would I take pleasure in your pain?**

SnowAngel: oh c'mon. because I am giving you permission to
take pleasure in my pain! to make your pain go
away!

zoegirl: **I don't think it works that way.**

Wed, Oct 2, 10:35 PM E.D.T.

SnowAngel: oy! I am such a cuckoo!

SnowAngel: I forgot to thank u both for the chocolates, u dear
sweet dearies!

mad maddie: **yr welcome. it was Zoe's idea.**

mad maddie: **Zo, u there?**

SnowAngel: she's prolly gone to bed.

mad maddie: **what the . . . ? it's seven thirty!**

SnowAngel: in California, ya show-off. in Zoe Land, as I
understand it, bedtime is promptly at 10 pm so that
she can get a full eight hours of sleep before waking
up at 6:30.

mad maddie: **why the hell does she get up at 6:30?**

SnowAngel: so she can make it to her 8 am class

mad maddie: **why the hell does she need an hour and a half to
get ready?**

SnowAngel: shower, shave, moisturize. blow-dry hair. pick cute
outfit. put on makeup. it's all about good hygiene,
Miz Mads.

mad maddie: **good hygiene is overrated.**

mad maddie: **so is doing laundry. HATE doing laundry. had no
idea how much till now.**

SnowAngel:	I so hear you. there's a girl in my pledge class who mails her dirty laundry home and then her mom mails it back all fresh and clean.
mad maddie:	that is ridiculous
mad maddie:	is that girl you?
SnowAngel:	ha ha, vair funny
mad maddie:	one moment, plz. must curse at the change machine for once again failing to accept my dollar bill.
SnowAngel:	hey, do u have a special laundry bag for yr intimates?
mad maddie:	hubba-wha?
SnowAngel:	yr lingerie, silly
mad maddie:	ohhhhh. you mean my thong made of pearls and my nipple-baring bra.
SnowAngel:	*eyes widen to saucers*
SnowAngel:	Maddie! I will be SO IMPRESSED if you really own those things. do you?
mad maddie:	no, fool
SnowAngel:	I think you shld invest in both. I truly do.
mad maddie:	and I will definitely positively absolutely keep that in mind.
mad maddie:	but only if the nipple-baring bra has cute straps
SnowAngel:	boom! YES! 😃

Thu, Oct 3, 9:05 PM E.D.T.

SnowAngel:	bork! bork bork BORK! 😠
zoegirl:	bork?
SnowAngel:	Lucy stole my chocolates!
zoegirl:	the ones we sent you? no way.
zoegirl:	she didn't really, did she?
SnowAngel:	uh, yes, cuz she is evil and shld be sent to Urinetown. also this time I had a witness. his name is Reid, and

	he's an ubergeek—"Doctor Who" shirts, carries miniature U.S. Constitution in his backpack (!!!), etc.—and he's my personal sherpa cuz of my crutches and all.
zoegirl:	your "sherpa"?
SnowAngel:	yup. he's in my geology class and he saw me struggling with my stuff, and also my cute jacket with Buddha on it was tied around my waist but kept falling off, and so he jumped up and helped me. and he's been helping ever since!
SnowAngel:	he keeps telling me he doesn't have to.
SnowAngel:	*I* keep telling him he doesn't have to! ack!
SnowAngel:	but he insists. so what am I supposed to do? I mean, it's not like I have a golf cart, right?
zoegirl:	?????
SnowAngel:	or a Segway. THAT WLD BE SO AWESOME IF I HAD A SEGWAY!
SnowAngel:	oh! did you know that science classes have labs yr supposed to go to? and, like, your lab grade is factored into your overall grade?
SnowAngel:	geology, you so crazy!
zoegirl:	Angela, *you* are so crazy. are you on drugs?
SnowAngel:	pain meds, baby. nom nom nom.
zoegirl:	well, they're making you act weird
SnowAngel:	well, my FOOT still hurts, so be nice.
SnowAngel:	I can't remember if I took one or two, altho yr allowed to take two, don't worry. so I took another and now my thumbs are frickin HUGE.
SnowAngel:	wait
SnowAngel:	sending pic
SnowAngel:	aren't they HUGE?
zoegirl:	you put your finger over the lens.
SnowAngel:	I did?

SnowAngel:	WHOA MY FINGER IS HUGE TOO!
zoegirl:	and if you haven't been going to your geology lab, then you need to go talk to your professor.
SnowAngel:	that's what Reid said! you and Reid are let's-say-the-same-thing twins!
zoegirl:	Reid, your sherpa? is that who we're talking about?
SnowAngel:	he is so dorky *giggle giggle*
SnowAngel:	he uses words like igneous and sedi-something-ary. he uses no hair product, he's never heard of J Brand *or* rag & bone, and he's actually been to UGA's library. like, more than once.
zoegirl:	I go to Kenyon's library all the time. Holly and I go there to study.
zoegirl:	Holly also randomly reshelves books. she finds it amusing.
SnowAngel:	one of my labia is significantly bigger than the other. SIGNIFICANTLY.
zoegirl:	WHAT?
SnowAngel:	I happened to notice and I thought I wld share. is there a problem?
zoegirl:	is anyone with you right now? like, watching after you?
SnowAngel:	I didn't notice just NOW, you perv. I noticed when I was shaving.
zoegirl:	seriously. you're not in your room alone, are you?
SnowAngel:	omg, you are so random!
SnowAngel:	REID IS HERE. he walked me to my dorm room after class, as I said, and as I also said, Reid is an ubergeek, so I had to hold my chin high and tell myself not to care what anyone thought.
zoegirl:	put Reid on the phone, please.
SnowAngel:	and when we got here, guess what? guess who was on *my* side of the room? YUP, IT WAS LUCY, which is how I know she stole my chocolates.

zoegirl:	yeah, because that's a totally logical assumption to make.
zoegirl:	but I'm not worried about your chocolates. I'm worried about you.
SnowAngel:	why???
SnowAngel:	and maybe I wld go to UGA's library—maybe—if the librarians wld change the no-phone rule. "cell-free zone"? who comes up with such nonsense?
zoegirl:	Angela? you need to lie down. you need to lie down and drink water.
SnowAngel:	whoa. I am suddenly very dizzy.
SnowAngel:	I need to lie down.
zoegirl:	do—and tell Reid to take care of you!

Thu, Oct 3, 9:47 PM E.D.T.

zoegirl:	are you worried about Angela?
zoegirl:	because I am. she parties all the time, she drinks too much, and she kisses boys whose names she doesn't even know. now she's abusing her Vicodin prescription, and not to sound melodramatic, but what if something bad happens?
mad maddie:	something more than poking a hole in her foot?
zoegirl:	out of all the kids we went to high school with, I didn't think Angela would be the biggest partier once we were in college.
mad maddie:	she's not. I saw on Susie Smith's FB page that Jana got so drunk that she had to have her stomach pumped. she had to be taken to the ER.
zoegirl:	see? and what if that happened to Angela? so scary!
mad maddie:	well, but Jana was always off the deep end. it's not like this is something new.
zoegirl:	will you talk to Angela? she would listen to you

more than she would to me, because she already thinks I'm a goody-goody.

mad maddie: u *are* a goody-goody.

mad maddie: also yr prolly overreacting, cuz college is just . . . college. it's its own bizarre world.

zoegirl: it's not supposed to be a stomach-pumping world, though

mad maddie: ok, I'll grant you that. but Angela didn't have to have her stomach pumped, did she?

mad maddie: and to put things in perspective, let me tell you about MY life. this morning I woke up to see Zara's friend Neesa lying buck naked on Zara's bed.

zoegirl: what?

mad maddie: buck naked! ON TOP OF THE COVERS!

zoegirl: ew! was she ok?

mad maddie: she was fine. she just sleeps in the buff. says it's the Cali way.

zoegirl: ew again. does Zara sleep naked?

mad maddie: no. t-shirt and boxers, praise the lord. (god, California is messing with my head!)

zoegirl: why was Neesa in Zara's bed instead of Zara?

mad maddie: girl, there's a relentless rotation of ppl in our room, except for me. I stay put.

zoegirl: huh

zoegirl: I'm trying to figure out how I feel about this.

mad maddie: I am too. constantly.

zoegirl: was she drunk?

mad maddie: when she crashed? dunno.

zoegirl: and she wasn't under the covers even a little bit? even just, like, part of the sheet?

mad maddie: nope, and when she woke up this morning, she just stretched her arms wide and yawned. no shyness or embarrassment or anything.

mad maddie: one part of me says, hell, it's her choice, and

	there's nothing WRONG with nakedness. theoretically.
mad maddie:	another part of me says that I didn't really want to see that.
zoegirl:	I wldn't either. sorry you had to deal with that, Mads.
mad maddie:	as am I.
mad maddie:	and I'll talk to Angela, sure. but as she has yet to show up naked on someone's bed, I'm not going to worry about her too much. she'll be ok.

Fri, Oct 4, 11:11 AM E.D.T.

SnowAngel:	hello, you two. my tongue feels too big for my mouth and my breath stinks and I suspect rotten zombies have taken residence in my gut.
SnowAngel:	that Vicodin made me CONK, I'll tell u.
SnowAngel:	must go brush my teeth or they will have to fumigate the whole dorm. also I need to erase a teeny-tiny oopsie of a lie I might have told.
SnowAngel:	apparently, Lucy *didn't* finish off my box of chocolates. apparently I did. or so says Reid.
SnowAngel:	but Lucy is still a thief, cuz she still stole the Q-tips, the conditioner, and the cotton balls.
SnowAngel:	did I tell y'all about the cotton balls? and at least five of my Express Cleansing Wipes and a BIG dollop of moisturizer.
SnowAngel:	I shld get a nanny cam!

Fri, Oct 4, 4:25 PM E.D.T.

zoegirl:	you guys! Doug is driving up to visit me tonight! HE suggested it, and HE'S making it happen, and I was worried for no good reason!!!
SnowAngel:	Zoe! that is WONDERFUL! *happy dance, happy dance*

SnowAngel:	oh, I'm so glad. phew!
zoegirl:	yes. PHEW. I think the strangeness between us WAS just growing pains. probably every couple has them, every couple but Maddie and Ian.
SnowAngel:	and they're so perfect together it makes me want to puke. 😊
SnowAngel:	all those sweet FB posts and tumblr pages! adorbs!
mad maddie:	the word "adorbs" makes me want to puke.
mad maddie:	and hello, ladies! I might pop in and out of convo cuz I'm in class, altho it is very much class-according-to-Santa-Cruz.
mad maddie:	prof had us meet outside, so I'm typing from under a zillion hundred-year-old redwoods. when I look up, all I can see are pockets of sky. I am a tiny little ant, and the world is insanely big.
zoegirl:	what class?
mad maddie:	intro to philosophy. we're all just kind of . . . philosophizing.
SnowAngel:	so how *are* things b/w you and Ian? has the long-distance thing been hard for y'all at all?
mad maddie:	r u insane? of course. I miss Ian all the time, I think about him all the time, I want to be with him all the time.
zoegirl:	except when you are doing the cool things you do with Zara and the Esbees, right? your life is totally an adventure, and for the record, I am continually trying to be more like you.
mad maddie:	well . . . thx, I guess.
zoegirl:	I'm trying to get out there more, and it's kind of working, but I seriously would like to know how you and Ian are holding so strong.
mad maddie:	we Skype a lot. we study together when we can, and we try to always have a face-to-face good-

	night, even if I have to take my laptop into the lounge for privacy.
zoegirl:	Doug and I Skype, but not that much.
mad maddie:	Ian wears honest-to-god pajamas, btw. striped ones with pants and a button-up pajama shirt. he says the guys on his hall give him hell.
SnowAngel:	I bet! but I'm sure he looks super-cute.
mad maddie:	he wears them ironically. for the record.
zoegirl:	maybe I need to Skype with Doug more.
zoegirl:	maybe I need to buy him pajamas . . .
SnowAngel:	*lifts eyebrows*
SnowAngel:	Skype away, but it wld be creepy to try to turn Doug into Ian.
zoegirl:	I didn't mean it like that.
zoegirl:	GROAN
mad maddie:	hey. don't worry about any of that when yr with Doug tonight. just relax and enjoy!!!

Fri, Oct 4, 7:30 PM E.D.T.

SnowAngel:	ladies!
SnowAngel:	THE WEEK OF CHEESE AND BREAD IS OVER! 🍾
SnowAngel:	raise yr glasses for me. No. More. Cheese! 🍺

Sat, Oct 5, 12:01 PM P.D.T.

mad maddie:	I am here to tell u that there truly are banana slugs all over UCSC's campus. u heard it here first, lady. 🐌 🌀
SnowAngel:	yay!
SnowAngel:	banana slugs are UCSC's mascot, right?
mad maddie:	yah, and they're actually kind of gross. they leave trails of slug-slime behind them. also, they're way bigger than I imagined.
SnowAngel:	as big as a banana? 😁

mad maddie:	smaller than a banana, bigger than . . .
mad maddie:	eh, who cares
mad maddie:	made me think of high school, tho, and applying to colleges, since that's when I first learned about banana slugs.
mad maddie:	that world seems so far away. remember how important Jana Whitaker was to us? and Zoe—ha! how she hid in the back of Jana's car to steal her teddy bear?
SnowAngel:	Boo Boo Bear! aw, good ol' Boo Boo Bear.
mad maddie:	do u follow Jana on Twitter or anything?
SnowAngel:	me? no.
SnowAngel:	why?
mad maddie:	oh, cuz of the stomach-pumping thing. did Zoe tell you about that? I'm wondering if she's ok, believe it or not.
SnowAngel:	yeah. hold on . . .
SnowAngel:	*mad Twitter activity*
SnowAngel:	kk, I am now officially following her. but you know, you *cld* follow her yrself
mad maddie:	except then she'd see me in her list of followers. no thx.
SnowAngel:	but you have no problem with her knowing that I'm following her?
mad maddie:	I don't want her to think I'm lame.
SnowAngel:	but it's fine for her to think I'm lame?
SnowAngel:	ooo! ooo! she just posted something!
SnowAngel:	wow, so deep. she said, "if yr not moving forward, yr falling behind. go back to high school, losah."
mad maddie:	you're moving forward. don't worry.
SnowAngel:	of course I'm moving forward. why wldn't I be moving forward? and why "don't worry"?
SnowAngel:	WAIT. she's not saying that to *me*, is she?
mad maddie:	one beat . . .

mad maddie: two beats . . .

SnowAngel: oh my god! she was, cuz she posted it the microsecond after I started following her!

mad maddie: she's JANA. did u really think she'd change?

mad maddie: u gave her an opening, and she slipped right back into high school.

mad maddie: or not. maybe high school came with her.

SnowAngel: huh?

mad maddie: sometimes I think I ran away from high school just to end up right back in high school, only now it's called college.

mad maddie: DON'T tweet her back!

Sat, Oct 5, 4:54 PM E.D.T.

SnowAngel: Zoe! how's the Dougster? ya gettin' some, know what I mean, know what I mean?

SnowAngel: Zoe! oohhhhh, Zoe!

SnowAngel: ALWAYS WEAR A CONDOM!

Sat, Oct 5, 6:30 PM E.D.T.

SnowAngel: Maaaaaaddddddiieeeee, Zoe won't answer my texts and won't pick up when I call. I feel neglected!

mad maddie: leave her be, fool.

mad maddie: stalker!

SnowAngel: also I told her to wear a condom, but really I meant that Doug shld wear a condom. on his penis. do you think she figured that out?

mad maddie: hmm. that's a tough one.

SnowAngel: Doug's penis? you're saying Doug's penis is a tough one???

SnowAngel: YOU'RE the stalker, weirdo!

Sun, Oct 6, 9:34 AM E.D.T.

zoegirl: Maddie, I'm sure you're still asleep.

zoegirl:	Angela, you probably are too.
zoegirl:	but . . .
zoegirl:	Doug broke up with me. he didn't come to visit me; he came to break up with me face-to-face.
zoegirl:	God, I never in my life thought I wld be typing these words.
zoegirl:	I wish I could hit "undo."

Sun, Oct 6, 11:00 AM E.D.T.

SnowAngel:	Zoe, wtf?
SnowAngel:	when? just now? do you want me to drive to Ohio and be with you??? I wld if I cld, you know!
zoegirl:	I'm numb. I'm a ghost. my skin is such an ugly color.
SnowAngel:	Zoe. no. you are not a ghost, and yr skin is beautiful. ALL of you is beautiful. don't you dare talk yrself into thinking this happened cuz something's wrong with you.
zoegirl:	he said he wants the full college experience. that he wants to experience new things. he said he didn't mean for his feelings toward me to change, but that they did.
SnowAngel:	my heart is breaking for you. I am SOOOOOO sorry!
zoegirl:	I can't think straight.
zoegirl:	this *is* really happening, right? I'm not dreaming?
SnowAngel:	shit, it's not that Canyon girl, is it?
zoegirl:	he claims they're just friends. I don't know.
zoegirl:	want to hear the worst part?
zoegirl:	well, all of it is the worst part, but at the end of his speech, he said, "so, uh, ok. I guess I'm going to take off."
SnowAngel:	when? this morning?
zoegirl:	um . . . not exactly

SnowAngel:	then when, exactly?
zoegirl:	on Friday night, right after he got here.
SnowAngel:	AND YOU'RE JUST NOW TELLING ME?
SnowAngel:	Zoe! wtf?!!!
zoegirl:	I was a mess, and I didn't want him to go, so I grabbed his hands and said, "it's late. just stay, please? you can drive back tomorrow."
SnowAngel:	okaaaay. and . . . ?
zoegirl:	he didn't want to, but I forced him to by being needy. and then he didn't want to sleep in my bed—he said he'd take the floor—but I was needy all over again until finally he gave in.
SnowAngel:	uh-oh
zoegirl:	yeah. so there we were in my bed, and our bodies were so close, and . . . things happened. except that's me not telling the whole truth, because I *made* them happen, just like when I visited him at Oberlin.
SnowAngel:	you made bad sex happen again? WHY?
zoegirl:	Angela! are you really asking that when you already know I feel like complete and utter shit?
SnowAngel:	sorry, sorry. bad phrasing!!!
SnowAngel:	let me try again. did Doug STOP things from happening? the "why look, here we are about to have sex again" things?
zoegirl:	no. but right before he came inside me, he whispered, "just so you know, this isn't going to change anything."
SnowAngel:	oh, Zoe. 😞
SnowAngel:	and Doug! what a fucker!
zoegirl:	so that's who I am, the girl who sleeps with her ex-boyfriend one last time even though she knows it's not going to change anything.
SnowAngel:	Zoe, that is NOT who you are

zoegirl:	well, um, it is. go me!
SnowAngel:	where are you now? are you in yr dorm room? I know yr not going to want to, but you need to be with other ppl right now. can you call your friend Holly?
zoegirl:	I just want to be alone.
SnowAngel:	and hold on. I'm confused.
SnowAngel:	today's Sunday. Doug broke up with you on Friday. Did he leave on Saturday?
zoegirl:	bright and early, yep
SnowAngel:	and you kept all this to yourself until now???
zoegirl:	I didn't feel like talking. or moving. or thinking. I still don't.
zoegirl:	will you tell Maddie for me? I don't want to do the walk of shame twice.
SnowAngel:	of course, but there is NO WALK OF SHAME.
SnowAngel:	I'm sending all my love!!!!!!!!!!!!!!!!!!

Sun, Oct 6, 7:28 PM P.D.T.

mad maddie:	hey, you.
SnowAngel:	hey. poor Zo, huh?
mad maddie:	I called her after you and I talked, but I got her voicemail. tried her again, got her voicemail again.
SnowAngel:	same here.
SnowAngel:	her latest tweet says, "gone off the grid. back eventually. #maybe."
mad maddie:	ack, I hear that
SnowAngel:	huh?
SnowAngel:	our friend is hurting and in pain and you're glad she's "gone off the grid"???
mad maddie:	what? no, I'm not glad! I said NOTHING about being glad.
mad maddie:	just, I understand the impulse.

SnowAngel:	what impulse?
mad maddie:	to go off the grid, even if you don't like that expression. to just . . . not deal.
SnowAngel:	but we're her friends! we're supposed to HELP her deal!
mad maddie:	yes. I know. and we will. I feel just as bad for Zoe as you do.
mad maddie:	I'm just acknowledging the fact that sometimes, when crappy things happen, it's tempting to disappear for a while.
SnowAngel:	*narrows eyes*
mad maddie:	and again, I'm not saying we're going to LET Zoe disappear. but don't you ever feel like you're constantly "on"? like you're chained to your phone/tablet/laptop/whatever? like you cldn't escape even if you wanted to?
SnowAngel:	as in, do I obsessively check for texts, emails, tweets, snapchats, and FB posts?
SnowAngel:	NO
mad maddie:	I do. sometimes I want to smash the internet with a rock. then I remember that y'all live in there, so I don't.
SnowAngel:	hmmph
mad maddie:	and now off to a diner on the boardwalk that serves maple bacon donut dogs.
mad maddie:	let me say that again: Maple. Bacon. Donut. Dogs.
SnowAngel:	that sounds revolting
mad maddie:	by which you mean "delicious beyond belief"? agreed. I shld buy a dozen and mail them to Zoe.
SnowAngel:	are Zara and the Esbees going with you?
mad maddie:	ish
SnowAngel:	they're going with you "ish"? I don't even know what that means.
mad maddie:	so don't worry about it

SnowAngel:	as for me, I'm txting from smelly laundry room in smelly dorm. (not my dorm.) Sunday night keg party, baby!
mad maddie:	**if you're at a keg party, why are you hiding in the smelly laundry room?**
SnowAngel:	eh. party is fun, but SO MUCH DRUNKENNESS!
mad maddie:	**then leave**
SnowAngel:	don't be silly! my constant companion, Reid, is here with me, and we're having a delightful conversation.
mad maddie:	**um, no. you're texting me.**
SnowAngel:	but he's holding my crutches. that's nice, isn't it?
SnowAngel:	I'm sitting on one of the washing machines.
mad maddie:	**and Reid's just standing there watching you???**
SnowAngel:	AND HOLDING MY CRUTCHES! omg, are you not listening?
mad maddie:	**is that sweet or creepy?**
SnowAngel:	it's sweet, dummy!
mad maddie:	**hmmm. in that case, I like Reid. tell him to keep taking care of you.**
SnowAngel:	ok, hold on . . .
SnowAngel:	Reid sez it is his pleasure and honor.
mad maddie:	**uh-oh. leaning back toward creepy . . .**
mad maddie:	**is he after yr body?**
SnowAngel:	no
mad maddie:	**are you after HIS body?**
SnowAngel:	plz! not in a million years.
mad maddie:	**why not? cuz he's a geek?**
SnowAngel:	he's not my type, that's all
mad maddie:	**why not? cuz he's a geek?**
SnowAngel:	Maddie, let's review:
SnowAngel:	Reid's an engineering major. his favorite class is optics, which I don't even know what that is, and he thinks it's a crime against the universe that I haven't

seen all the "Star Wars" movies. (and he has slightly acne-scarred skin, and it's not terrible, but . . . yeah.)

mad maddie: **ahhhh. so you're just using him to lug around your crutches and watch you text ppl.**

SnowAngel: stop trying to make me feel bad!

SnowAngel: I like him—as a FRIEND—but he's not in a fraternity. I know you won't understand, but at UGA, Greeks are expected to date Greeks.

mad maddie: **I think I'm going to vomit**

SnowAngel: wow. thx. vomit away, Mads. vomit all over yr stupid hot dog donut!!!

Sun, Oct 6, 11:28 PM P.D.T.

mad maddie: **as it turns out, I did not spend my night vomiting all over my donut.**

mad maddie: **I rescued a tiger instead. *blows casually on fingernails***

mad maddie: **not a fully grown tiger, obviously. a cub. a cub named Chewy.**

mad maddie: **I won't bore you with all the deets, but a friend of Zara's named Tom was keeping Chewy in his apartment, only he wasn't supposed to be, cuz, ya know, tigers aren't allowed in apartments, and also Tom wasn't Chewy's real owner.**

mad maddie: **point is, Tom had to return Chewy to the real owner dude, so we volunteered to help.**

mad maddie: **you're thinking, "why is Maddie telling me all this," right?**

mad maddie: **I have to tell someone, cuz I got the piss scared out of me.**

mad maddie: **Chewy was just a cub, sure. BUT HE WAS STILL A TIGER. and rescuing a tiger—even being that close to a tiger—made me re-realize how much I want my time on earth to *mean* something.**

mad maddie: there's this dead guy we're learning about in my philosophy class, and he describes life as "solitary, poor, nasty, brutish, and short." now there's a Hallmark card slogan, huh?

mad maddie: but I think he's full of it. I think life could be any of those things, but it's up to us to make sure it isn't.

mad maddie: meaning, I didn't go out tonight expecting any kind of danger. at all. but say something had gone wrong—melodramatic, I know—but what if something *did* happen to me, and the last convo you and I ever had ended in a fight?

mad maddie: (a DUMB fight, and I was a jerk, and I'm sorry.)

mad maddie: Angela, you and Zoe mean the world to me. Santa Cruz is AWESOME, der, but y'all are awesomer.

mad maddie: anyway . . .

mad maddie: I'll probably keep giving you a hard time about stuff, but I won't threaten to vomit on you anymore.

mad maddie: forgive?

Mon, Oct 7, 7:35 AM E.D.T.

SnowAngel: holy fuck, Maddie! YOU ARE INSANE!

SnowAngel: not that I'm surprised, but oh. my. god. your life is like a movie, you crazy girl.

SnowAngel: call me the second you wake up! I am ordering you to!

SnowAngel: and I'm going to let you tell Zo, not me. if you haven't already. it'll mean more that way, esp the part about how we're the ones responsible for how our lives turn out. like maybe it'll help with her Doug sadness?

SnowAngel: or not.

SnowAngel: but, eek

SnowAngel: chills

SnowAngel: I don't know if you're my hero or just my dumbass BFF, but yes, all is forgiven. GAH!!!!!

Mon, Oct 7, 1:01 PM E.D.T.

zoegirl: college so far:

zoegirl: you: parties, parties, parties. hole in foot. emergency room. business class that you don't hate, much to your surprise. cute geeky boy who adores you, even if you don't adore him back.

SnowAngel: it's not that I don't adore him. just not as a boyfriend.

zoegirl: Maddie: adventure-time city including exotic animals.

SnowAngel: hahahahaha, I know! 🐯

zoegirl: me? pathetic and lonely and can't stop thinking about Doug. I'm a broken heart collecting dust.

SnowAngel: you don't have to be. you cld have adventures too, and it wld take your mind off stupid Doug.

SnowAngel: you cld liberate a boa constrictor! hahahaha!

zoegirl: bye, Angela

SnowAngel: you cld at least try

SnowAngel: YOU CLD AT LEAST LIBERATE A GERBIL!!!!

Mon, Oct 7, 5:55 PM P.D.T.

mad maddie: hey, girl. just checking in on you like I said I wld. doing any better?

zoegirl: no

zoegirl: all day I kept expecting Doug to call and say what a terrible mistake he'd made, but guess what? he didn't.

mad maddie: cuz he's an idiot. we've gone over this.

zoegirl: how can I still love him when he doesn't love me? how is it possible for me to feel SO MUCH and for him to feel nothing?

mad maddie:	he's not feeling "nothing." he's being a dumbshit and I want to punch him in the face, but I'm sure he's struggling too.
zoegirl:	riiiight. that's why his FB status was all about how he bought an electric guitar and is going to be the next Les Paul.
mad maddie:	oh, gag
mad maddie:	what guy doesn't want to play the electric guitar and become crazy famous?
mad maddie:	and who the hell is Les Paul?
zoegirl:	he's the guy who invented the electric guitar, back in the fifties. I Googled him.
mad maddie:	double gag. what a show-off.
zoegirl:	I know. I'm sure he's trying to impress his fancy friends at Oberlin.
mad maddie:	like Canyon?
zoegirl:	fuck Canyon. no doubt Doug is.
mad maddie:	ouch
mad maddie:	I don't think I've ever heard you say that word before.
zoegirl:	people change (obviously)
zoegirl:	I skipped all my classes today too.
mad maddie:	whoa. the universe is imploding. THIS GOES AGAINST ALL NATURAL LAWS.
mad maddie:	what next? are you going to drop out, live in the woods, and start growing your own food?
zoegirl:	maybe
mad maddie:	oh, plz
mad maddie:	college is overrated, I'll give u that. but Zoe, you were *made* for college and you know it!

Tues, Oct 8, 2:22 PM E.D.T.

zoegirl:	Zone bars have 19 vitamins and minerals, 14

	grams of protein, and 7 grams of fat. did you know that?
SnowAngel:	that's a lot of fat . . .
SnowAngel:	then again, a Zone bar is supposed to be an entire meal, isn't it? that's one of the marketing strategies for nutrition/energy bars. learned that in my business class.
SnowAngel:	(for me, however, that strategy is a fail. I don't want an energy bar for a meal. I want a MEAL for a meal.)
zoegirl:	also, one bar provides 35% of the daily recommended amount of molybdenum.
SnowAngel:	well, duh
zoegirl:	so if I eat three a day, I'm all set. I don't ever have to leave my room again.
SnowAngel:	Zoe. dearest. you know I love you, but you can't stay holed up in yr room just because Doug broke up with you.
zoegirl:	for what it's worth, I *think* about leaving my room. I visualize myself getting up and doing it, but . . . I don't know. something fizzles out and I stay stuck on my bed.
zoegirl:	I just keep wondering what I did wrong to make Doug stop loving me. what did I do wrong, Angela?
SnowAngel:	remember the guy my Aunt Sadie dated over the summer? the guy she met on match.com?
zoegirl:	the architect?
SnowAngel:	yeah. his name was Bill, and she really liked him, and she *thought* he really liked her, and then out of the blue, he totally broke things off.
zoegirl:	does this story have a happy ending?
SnowAngel:	Aunt Sadie was really sad, so her friends came over

with wine, and she let me have a glass, and it was yummy.

SnowAngel: BUT. one of her friends said that women believe that if they love someone as hard as they can, they'll get back love in the same degree. only it doesn't work that way, cuz love isn't like a math equation where two plus two always equals four.

zoegirl: **but two plus two does equal four.**

SnowAngel: in Math Land, but not in Love Land.

SnowAngel: like, Aunt Sadie assumed that Bill really really liked her because she really really liked him. only he didn't. it wasn't anyone's fault. he just didn't.

zoegirl: **but Doug . . .**

SnowAngel: what you two had was real. I'm not saying it wasn't.

SnowAngel: but things changed. it wasn't anybody's fault, and god, Zoe, you didn't do anything *wrong*. things just . . . changed. and I don't want to sound harsh, but hiding out in your room isn't going to change them back.

SnowAngel: does that sound awful? am I being a terrible friend?

zoegirl: **no**

zoegirl: **I'm sure you're right. I just don't like it.** 😔

SnowAngel: oh, sweetie. I know.

SnowAngel: but will you plz get up and leave yr room? and take a shower, and eat, and be around ppl? it'll make u feel so much better, I promise.

zoegirl: **I'll think about it.**

zoegirl: **but I'd rather two plus two go back to equaling four.**

Wed, Oct 9, 6:01 PM P.D.T.

mad maddie: **I told Zoe that she has till the end of the week to feel sorry for herself, but after that she has to get off her butt and get back in the game.**

mad maddie: that's what I do when I'm depressed. I let myself sulk for an hour or a day or whatever, and then I say, "ok, enough."

SnowAngel: an hour or a day? hahaha. or a week or a month or a year . . .

mad maddie: don't be mean. c'mon, even you get depressed sometimes.

SnowAngel: hmm. I'm not happy every minute of every day, true. but most of the time I kind of am.

SnowAngel: also, I think I get grumpy instead of depressed—and instead of moping, I share my grumpy feelings with y'all! because I love you! 😀

mad maddie: whereas I just shove my unwanted feelings under the rug and pretend everything's hunky-dory. 😊

SnowAngel: silly Maddie. everying IS hunky-dory!

SnowAngel: wanna hear a cute story about Reid that made me think of you?

mad maddie: why does Reid make you think of me?

SnowAngel: he doesn't. shush and listen.

mad maddie: yes ma'am

SnowAngel: earlier tonight, I had an insane craving for an almond croissant, which doesn't sound like me, I know. but college changes a girl.

mad maddie: ah. such wisdom.

SnowAngel: I know, right?

SnowAngel: so Reid said he'd go get me one. only he doesn't have a car, so he had to bike to the bakery that sells them, only he got there just after they closed. boo!

SnowAngel: sooooo, Reid biked to Dunkin' Donuts, which is on the completely opposite side of town from the bakery, and he bought me a dozen donuts. wasn't that sweet? and do you understand now why it made me think of you? cuz of the donuts!

mad maddie: what flave?

SnowAngel: an assortment, since he didn't know what my favorite was. he brought them to me at the Zeta house, and I shared them with my sorority sisters, and everyone was like, "awww, what a cutie-pie. he shld be our mascot." and . . . yeah.

mad maddie: wow. that must have made him feel manly.

SnowAngel: I hear that tone you're using! you are judging me and assuming I'm using Reid or whatever, when really what you shld be noticing is that I invited him TO THE ZETA HOUSE, which shows that I wasn't embarrassed of him. isn't that good?

mad maddie: you permitted him to come to your sorority house bearing fried delicacies. you're a peach, all right.

mad maddie: did you give him a blow job to express your gratitude?

SnowAngel: gross!!!!

SnowAngel: no, I did not, and you're missing the point. I am simply admitting that YES, I LIKE REID. I'm not saying he's boyfriend material, but the little fella's growing on me.

mad maddie: Angela? if one person mentions a blow job, and the other person responds by saying, "the little fella's growing on me . . ."

SnowAngel: omg

mad maddie: hot tip: if you stroke the little fella, the little fella will grow and grow until—hopefully—he's a big, firm fella. then wld he be boyfriend material?

SnowAngel: SO inappro-pro. zero donuts for you, missy!!!

Wed, Oct 9, 6:38 PM P.D.T.

mad maddie: omg, lightning bolt: is Reid your new Logan? aka Boy Who Adores You Unquestioningly and

Thus You Tolerate Him and Secretly Give Him Unwarranted Hope?

SnowAngel: what? NO!

SnowAngel: Logan was a high school boy. I was a high school girl.

SnowAngel: NO, Reid is not a new Logan. and Maddie. ouch.

mad maddie: **but he does adore you unquestioningly**

SnowAngel: actually, for the record, he doesn't. hmmph.

mad maddie: **not to be skeptical, but really?**

SnowAngel: well, he does adore me, yes. *blushes modestly*

SnowAngel: but unlike Logan, he also gives me crap about stuff—like not going to my geology lab and how there's no reason for me to wear hard-to-walk-in skirts if I don't want to (I happened to mention one day how tricky miniskirts cld be) and things like that.

SnowAngel: also, he is very supportive of my business acumen (yes, acumen!) and makes me feel like I *could* be a businesswoman if I wanted to. one day. like, that I'm smart enough.

mad maddie: **of course you're smart enough, dum-dum. jeebus.**

SnowAngel: I'm just saying HE'S NOT LOGAN, cuz he sees *me* and not just silly cute giggly me. so there! 😊

Thu, Oct 10, 8:44 PM E.D.T.

SnowAngel: hi! *waves broadly*

SnowAngel: have you set yr reset button yet?

zoegirl: **no comment**

SnowAngel: well that's stupid

SnowAngel: wanna hear something else stupid?

SnowAngel: yesterday Maddie and I were talking about blow jobs (don't ask), and then tonight when I went to the Zeta house for dinner, the topic came up again.

zoegirl:	**don't really want to talk about blow jobs, Angela.**
SnowAngel:	sure ya do. unless—hint hint—you have something better to do . . . ?
zoegirl:	**fine, tell me**
SnowAngel:	I was sitting with some other pledges, and they said that the pledges in Sigma Phi were EXPECTED to give the guys in a certain fraternity blow jobs. like, expected to give blow jobs just the way they're expected to show up at chapter meetings.
SnowAngel:	don't you think that is SO wrong?
zoegirl:	**um, yeahhhhh. it can't be true, though. do you think it's true?**
SnowAngel:	I dunno, but if any of the actives asked me to do that? no ma'am and buh-bye. horrible, horrible, horrible.
zoegirl:	**what's an "active"?**
SnowAngel:	someone who's been initiated. in other words, not me, cuz I'm still a pledge.
SnowAngel:	another pledge at my table said that last week the Delta Theta pledges had to dress like hos and walk the streets of downtown Athens for three hours.
zoegirl:	**ugh**
SnowAngel:	I know. compared with giving blow jobs and being hos, eating cheese sandwiches for a week was nothing.
zoegirl:	**do you know any girls from those other sororities personally?**
SnowAngel:	ha. no.
SnowAngel:	I haven't even learned the names of all the Zetas, altho I better, cuz at some point we're going to be given a pop quiz. rewards if we ace it, punishment if we don't.
zoegirl:	**what would the reward be?**
SnowAngel:	probably candy. we usually have our pledge class

	meetings on the back porch, and Natalia, our pledge class leader, throws candy at us afterward.
zoegirl:	**candy? I thought sorority girls were supposed to be skinny.**
SnowAngel:	huh. we are. that's weird that they wld throw candy at us, then, isn't it?
zoegirl:	**so what would the punishment be? although I'm scared to ask.**
SnowAngel:	oh, we'd have to clean up the house, or maybe just the bathrooms. or if only one girl fails, she might have to be a personal assistant for one of the older Zetas for a week. something like that.
SnowAngel:	I have one last horror story for you. there's a girl in my pledge class named Brittney, and she told us that her big sister (her REAL big sister, as in yes, they grew up together and have the same parents) went to Florida State.
SnowAngel:	Brittney's sister was in a sorority for a while, but she dropped out when she found out about a tradition one of the FSU frats had.
SnowAngel:	supposedly the fraternity pledges had to prove their manhood by asking a girl to a house party and getting her wasted by slipping a roofie into her drink. then he'd take her to a "special room" and have sex with her, even if she was passed out.
zoegirl:	**Angela. that's rape.**
SnowAngel:	just wait. the special room had a big glass window with a wide ledge beneath it, and the other guys in the frat wld stand on the ledge and watch. they'd take pics, cheer the pledge on, whatever.
zoegirl:	**omigod**
SnowAngel:	uh-huh. they called those parties "ledge parties."
SnowAngel:	but that was at FSU. I've never heard of anything like that happening at UGA.

zoegirl: maybe I should have gone to a women's college.

zoegirl: maybe I should join a convent and dedicate my life to charity work.

SnowAngel: but where's the fun in that?

SnowAngel: SOME partying is good and healthy and normal, Zo. and some guys are dicks, but not all of them. not even most of them.

SnowAngel: do charity work later. right now you shld just enjoy yourself!!!

Thu, Oct 10, 9:20 PM E.D.T.

SnowAngel: how's tricks, gal pal? is there a stranger in yr bed and a pounding in yr head?

mad maddie: one sec. gotta swipe meal-plan card.

SnowAngel: I just changed the bandage on my foot—or rather, Reid did. it was nasty and involved ooze.

mad maddie: and it seems I'll be passing on the mashed potatoes and gravy I just paid for. thx, A.

SnowAngel: also you can totally still see the hole. it's starting to heal over, but if I wanted to, I bet I cld poke a pencil thru it.

mad maddie: you do that. enjoy!

Fri, Oct 11, 11:30 AM P.D.T.

mad maddie: wassup, doodie?

SnowAngel: "doodie"?

mad maddie: grrr. *doodie

mad maddie: *DUDE

mad maddie: fricking autocorrect!

SnowAngel: hee hee. I was txting my sister the other day, and she told me she loved her high school friends but hated all the homoeroticism.

mad maddie: ha!

SnowAngel: she meant homework. it made me laugh.

SnowAngel: and then this morning, I texted Aunt Sadie to get
               her advice about Reid. I wanted to know how to be
               his friend without leading him on, and she said that
               mainly I'd just have to curb my natural instinct to flirt
               with him.

mad maddie: is that possible? u flirt with everyone.

mad maddie: u flirt with trees, for heaven's sake

SnowAngel: that's what I told her! so she texted me back and
               said, "sweetheart, I'm not saying it'll be easy. but I
               promise you can't do it."

mad maddie: ha. so supportive.

SnowAngel: I was like, "Really, Aunt Sadie? You have THAT MUCH
               FAITH in me?"

SnowAngel: she had to reread our exchange to know what I was
               talking about, and then she was mortified.

**mad maddie: typing "can't" instead of "can" isn't an autocorrect,
               tho. just a typo.**

SnowAngel: whatev. still funny.

**mad maddie: my best/worst autocorrect was when I txted Ian
               the other day.**

SnowAngel: how is that cute Ian? I saw him for like ten minutes
               on the quad before I had to dash off to the Zeta
               house for lunch. he looked happy, tho. is he?

**mad maddie: I think so. he likes his roommate. he LOVES his
               engineering classes—and he knows Reid, btw.**

SnowAngel: I know! and they like each other—yay!

**mad maddie: and he plays Halo with a bunch of guys on his
               hall, and he says they're pretty cool, so yeah, I
               think he's having fun.**

SnowAngel: he misses you like crazy, I bet

mad maddie: yeah. well. we avoid that topic.

SnowAngel: why?

mad maddie: what do you mean, why?

mad maddie: what's the point of torturing ourselves by talking about something we can't have?

SnowAngel: 😔

SnowAngel: um, because sharing your feelings would make you feel better?

mad maddie: ohhhh

mad maddie: and what wld I say? that I wish I'd gone to UGA instead of Santa Cruz so that we cld hold hands and walk to class together and crawl into the same bed every night? that California is so much farther away than I thought? that without him, I feel like I'm dying inside?

SnowAngel: oh, Maddie ☹️

mad maddie: that's Zoe, not me. feeling sorry for yrself is an exercise in futility.

SnowAngel: but . . .

SnowAngel: argh. I knew you missed Ian—duh—but I had no idea how much. I mean, you're always talking about casinos and tigers and hot dog donuts. I just assumed you were having a super-fun time and that Santa Cruz was awesome.

mad maddie: I *am* having a super-fun time and SC *is* awesome, and I keep myself busy on purpose so that I can live in denial at the same time.

mad maddie: can we move on?

SnowAngel: but . . . but . . . I don't want you to feel like you're dying inside!

mad maddie: omg. and apparently I shldn't have told you, either.

mad maddie: do you want to hear my worst autocorrect or not?

SnowAngel: um, sure

mad maddie: you'll like it, I promise.

mad maddie: I sent Ian a text about scarfing down Flamin' Hot Cheetos and guzzling a Coke, but autocorrect decided I was guzzling a cock. 😳

SnowAngel: ha!

SnowAngel: bet Ian loved that. bet it made him wish you were there to guzzle HIS cock. 😊

mad maddie: Angela? to guzzle means "to drink greedily." (thank u, dictionary app)

SnowAngel: ok, then nuzzle! it's a good idea to NUZZLE a cock, isn't it?

mad maddie: only way to find out is to try. yr Aunt Sadie won't approve, but Reid will be thrilled. 😏

Sat, Oct 12, 2:01 PM E.D.T.

zoegirl: it's two o'clock on a Saturday, it's gorgeous outside, and yet here I am, sitting on my bed doing nothing.

mad maddie: urrrrgggghhhh. noooooooo.

zoegirl: I keep telling myself to get up and go for a walk, because I know it would make me feel better. but I can't. it's like I'm physically stuck.

zoegirl: it's actually kind of freaking me out

mad maddie: ZOE

mad maddie: do you think yr truly depressed? do you think you shld see a doctor?

zoegirl: I don't feel like *me*.

zoegirl: I know I was happy once, but I can't remember what it feels like.

mad maddie: ok, babes? yr scaring me, cuz YOU ARE A HAPPY PERSON. you're wired that way. and we've had so many happy times together!

zoegirl: yeah . . . ?

mad maddie: omg. YES. like the last week of high school, when we had the mud slide and you and Angela and I got soooo filthy. that was so. much. fun. you can remember that, can't u?

zoegirl: I can see it in my mind, but it's like . . .

zoegirl: it's like there's glass between me and that girl. I can remember the idea of being happy, but I can't remember the feeling.

mad maddie: maybe you shld go to Kenyon's health clinic. talk to a counselor or something.

zoegirl: boohoo, my high school boyfriend and I broke up in the first semester of college, just like everyone in the world said we would. so original.

mad maddie: who said you and Doug were going to break up?

zoegirl: oh, I don't know.

zoegirl: maybe no one said that specifically, but my parents said things like, "we like Doug very much, but don't limit yourself" and "most high school relationships don't last, you know. you need to prepare yourself for that possibility."

mad maddie: prepare yrself to have yr heart broken? that seems . . .

mad maddie: well, it seems cruel, almost. and how does focusing on the negative help? wldn't it be better to put a smile on and hope for the best?

zoegirl: that makes me think of Ian's last Instagram pic. the one of him making a heart with his hands with the caption "missing my girl." made me want to cry and smile at the same time.

mad maddie: I liked that one too. I have NOT been liking all the bleak landscape pics you've been posting.

zoegirl: that's what I see when I look out my window, so . . .

zoegirl: I'm following Zara now, btw.

mad maddie: Zara? as in my roommate Zara? you're following her on Instagram?

zoegirl: I found her on your profile page. you don't post enough pictures, and I wanted to learn more about your new California life.

zoegirl: I'm confused about one of the pictures she posted, though. the one of the bathroom in y'all's suite where it looks as if everyone doodles and writes notes on the tiles using Sharpies.

mad maddie: the RA doesn't care. Zara promised we'd clean it all off at the end of the year.

zoegirl: I don't care about that—and anyway, it's really cute, all those white tiles with smiley faces and hearts and peace signs drawn on them. and that dragon! whoever drew that dragon is GOOD.

zoegirl: but the notes say things like "Rock it, Z!" and "hugs to Neesa" and something about how Erica should call Frank "Francis"?

mad maddie: he's just a guy that hangs out with that group.

mad maddie: our group.

mad maddie: his real name is Francis. go fig.

zoegirl: ok, but why no "hugs to Maddie"?

zoegirl: why are there no notes to you at all?

mad maddie: that's a weird question

zoegirl: is it?

zoegirl: no notes from you either

mad maddie: well, Zoe, here is why. Zara's Instagram pic only shows two walls of the bathroom. two out of . . . I dunno, ten or twelve including the stalls and showers.

mad maddie: what did you think, that everyone in the suite decorated the bathroom except me?

zoegirl:	well . . . *shrugs*
mad maddie:	**omg, I'm so offended! or I wld be if I weren't laughing so hard.**
mad maddie:	**I've written stuff on the tiles too. they're just not in that pic.**
mad maddie:	**crazy girl!**

Sat, Oct 12, 5:13 PM E.D.T.

SnowAngel:	I just sat thru the WORST scolding of my life, you guys.
SnowAngel:	it was like being yelled at by Southern Belle Barbie meets Desperate Housewife from Hell, and you shld both feel sorry for me and offer to rub my bunions.
SnowAngel:	don't you feel sorry for me?
SnowAngel:	I don't actually have bunions.
SnowAngel:	I don't actually know what bunions are.
SnowAngel:	OMG, REALLY? where are you ppl when I need you?!!!
SnowAngel:	Tandy, the social chair of the Alpha Zetas, called an emergency pledge meeting because apparently sororities have emergencies involving social-ness.
SnowAngel:	here is the first thing she said once we were sitting down: "now listen, y'all. don't even THINK about moving your derrieres from this room until I'm done. you're all going to want to run away like little bitty babies because you're all in huge fucking trouble, but if you move even one of your ugly-ass butt cheeks? you. are. dead. y'all got that?"
SnowAngel:	it was half scary and half funny, but Tandy wasn't joking.
SnowAngel:	for the next hour, she told us we were the worst pledge class in the history of Alpha Zetas. that we don't show enough Zeta spirit, that we don't make a splash on campus, that we don't wear our letters

	enough, and that only HALF of us had purchased the Zeta lavaliers we're supposed to buy, and what the fuck was up with that?
SnowAngel:	a lavalier is a necklace with the Greek letters for whatever yr sorority is on it, in case you didn't know. I'm one of the girls who hasn't bought one, but not as an act of rebellion. just cuz I'm lazy.
SnowAngel:	see, you have to log on to this online store—there's Alpha Zeta comforters, Alpha Zeta mugs, Alpha Zeta teddy bears, Alpha Zeta undies . . . but something went wrong when I was creating my account and I cldn't get it to work and finally I said, screw it.
SnowAngel:	ANYway, after the lavalier rant, she told us that she'd gotten complaints from various frat guys about how "boring and lame" we are. wtf????
SnowAngel:	I am many things, but I am NOT boring or lame!
SnowAngel:	but Tandy was like, "lesson one, bitches: if frats don't like the fucking boring pledges they invite to parties, then they stop liking the sororities they belong to. y'all are making the rest of us look bad, so stop sucking ass and man up, you twats."
SnowAngel:	she really did use that word. I'm not kidding!
SnowAngel:	she also asked if we were fucking brain damaged.
SnowAngel:	the only thing that made Tandy's rant bearable was Anna, my best pledge-buddy. I 🖤 Anna. she kept making spit bubbles when Tandy wasn't looking, hee hee hee. and when I say spit bubbles, I mean real, live spit bubbles, not drool.
SnowAngel:	I have no idea how she does it, but she can make teeny-tiny little bubbles leave her lips and float thru the air.
SnowAngel:	amazebubbles!!!!
SnowAngel:	well, yeah, blah blah blah. when we were finally

allowed to leave, Anna and I went to Shakes Alive and talked about how cray-cray Tandy is and also about how cray-cray being in a sorority is, period. it's not all bad, and there are excellent parts as well as sucky parts, but I'm starting to wonder if it's going to be sorority-ever-after for me after all.

SnowAngel: Anna is too.

SnowAngel: oh, and Anna is super-cute, only I told her how she'd look even cuter if she used a slightly less red shade of lipgloss and swept her bangs to the side. (for the record, I ASKED if she wanted my extremely gentle tips, and she said yes, so stop thinking whatever you're thinking unless it's that I'm so awesome.)

SnowAngel: I also taught her the half-tuck, cuz she has a great body and shld show it off. and I'm gonna take her shopping for jeans, cuz the ones she has are fine but cld be so much better.

SnowAngel: so yeah, that's me. *blows invisible fashion-fairy dust off fingernails* adios, amigas!

Sun, Oct 13, 11:33 AM E.D.T.

zoegirl: thank you, Angela, for taking a poll on Twitter about whether or not I got out of bed today. that was lovely and heartwarming. it really was.

SnowAngel: hee hee 😄

SnowAngel: you know I was just being funny

zoegirl: well, joke's on you, cuz I not only got out of bed but also went for a jog. a *jog* jog, as in sneakers and huffing and puffing and making my feet move me from one place to another. it sucked, and I hated it, but now that it's over, I feel better than I've felt in forever.

SnowAngel: dude! dudette! you so beamin'!

SnowAngel:	is it like a runner's high?
zoegirl:	I don't know. maybe. I told myself I would jog the entire trail that loops around the campus (it's a mile and a half), and I didn't let myself stop even when I wanted to.
zoegirl:	and I really wanted to.
SnowAngel:	I'm so proud of you! taking a mile-and-a-half jog sounds terrible and horrible, but yay, you!
zoegirl:	I had a mantra that I repeated as I ran. it was "screw Doug. screw Doug. screw Doug." and maybe it was sort of like therapy, because a) it felt good to get those bad feelings out, and b) I was so spent afterward that I didn't have enough energy left to be depressed.
SnowAngel:	look at you go, girl! you have just earned five gold stars! ★ ★ ★ ★ ★
zoegirl:	I still miss him, though. I'm mad at him and I hate him (and I definitely hate Canyon!), but I miss him too.
SnowAngel:	but you don't miss Canyon.
zoegirl:	ha
zoegirl:	no, I don't miss Canyon. that made me snort.
zoegirl:	hey—what the hell is a half-tuck?
SnowAngel:	like what I taught Anna to do? you tuck in half of your shirt, like from your belly button to your hip, and you leave the rest hanging out. that way it shows that you still have a waist, but you don't look like the kind of person who tucks her shirts in on purpose.
SnowAngel:	casual + sexy, see? 😊
zoegirl:	ahhhhh. will keep that in mind.
zoegirl:	I'm stinky from my run so I'm going to take a shower.
SnowAngel:	kk. and again: you rock, girlfriend!

zoegirl:	hey, A. me again.
SnowAngel:	what happened to taking a shower?
zoegirl:	waiting in hall. I forgot that there's always a Sunday morning shower line. *facepalm*
SnowAngel:	cuz of all the Saturday night partying. boom!
zoegirl:	do you ever wonder if Maddie is as close as she says she is to Zara and her friends from high school?
SnowAngel:	the Esbees? um . . . no.
SnowAngel:	do u? 😐
zoegirl:	check out Maddie's Instagram if you haven't lately. I went to her profile and clicked to see who she was following, and one of the people was "themarkofzara."
SnowAngel:	I don't get it
zoegirl:	the mark of Zara. like the "Mark of Zorro"?
SnowAngel:	still don't get it
zoegirl:	doesn't matter. so I started following Zara, and guess what? she's posted TONS of pictures, but Maddie doesn't show up in a single one.
SnowAngel:	hmm
SnowAngel:	is that weird? I'm thinking about it, and I can't decide. I mean, I post tons of pics, but they're not all of my new UGA buds.
zoegirl:	Angela, yes they are. omigod. the ONLY pictures you post are sorority pics and party pics and drunkish party-outfit-posing pics.
SnowAngel:	not true!
SnowAngel:	maybe true.
SnowAngel:	ok, true, except don't forget my derpy puppies in a basket picture.
zoegirl:	I asked Maddie about it, and she said she just doesn't like having her picture taken.

SnowAngel:	she doesn't. remember her whole curl-up-in-a-ball/ hide-her-face-with-her-hands phase when either of us tried to take her pic?
zoegirl:	but she grew out of that phase
SnowAngel:	well, I don't know, then. I guess she grew back in.

Mon, Oct 14, 7:55 PM E.D.T.

zoegirl:	there is a pumpkin in our dining hall that weighs 1,400 pounds and is named Gourdzilla!
zoegirl:	it is so cool! 🎃
mad maddie:	that is one big pumpkin.
mad maddie:	how do u know it weighs that much?
zoegirl:	there's a sign. also I just now lifted it up, and by my guesstimate, that sounded about right.
mad maddie:	such a brute! I like! 💪
zoegirl:	Holly and Gannon and I held hands and tried to wrap our arms around her, but we didn't come close.
mad maddie:	her? the pumpkin has a vagina?
zoegirl:	no.
zoegirl:	well, not to my knowledge.
zoegirl:	but it's a tradition at Kenyon to have a gigantic pumpkin in the cafeteria to celebrate fall, and I guess the pumpkin is always a "she." that's how everyone refers to her.
zoegirl:	she's huge, Maddie. seriously, you would love her.
mad maddie:	snapchat?
zoegirl:	yes, ma'am . . .
mad maddie:	omfg, I LOVE THAT PUMPKIN. I want to eat that pumpkin and have that pumpkin's babies!
zoegirl:	the second pic is of Holly and Gannon. they both say hi.
mad maddie:	hi back

mad maddie: why is Holly's belly button green?

zoegirl: she got bored in one of her classes and colored it.

mad maddie: why is her belly button visible?

zoegirl: because she has her shirt tied back, silly!

zoegirl: kidding. I mean, it IS, but the "why" is because she wanted to show off her green belly button. she's hoping people will think it's mold.

mad maddie: well, she and Gannon both look nice.

zoegirl: they are. they were worried about me during my time in the Bad Lands too, as it turns out.

mad maddie: but yr better now?

zoegirl: yup. I went for a run again this morning, and I'm going to try to make myself do that three times a week. I'm not going to skip class anymore, and today I met with all my profs and asked if I could make up the work I missed.

zoegirl: my heart is still secretly hurting . . . but too bad.

mad maddie: fake it till ya make it?

zoegirl: yes. exactly.

zoegirl: and I'm not TOTALLY faking it. alone in my dorm room, I'm a pathetic self-pitying mess, but when I'm with other people, it's so much better.

mad maddie: which—ahem—I told you five million years ago

zoegirl: I know, I know.

zoegirl: so what'd you do over the weekend?

mad maddie: you have to ask? I sat alone in my dorm room like a pathetic self-pitying mess, obviously.

zoegirl: Maddie . . .

zoegirl: ☹

zoegirl: that was kind of mean. did you intend it to be?

mad maddie: I didn't. I'm sorry. the second I hit "send," I realized it wasn't a good joke.

zoegirl: it wasn't even a bad joke. ☹

mad maddie: yr right, and I really am sorry.

mad maddie: what I really did over the weekend—hold on to yer hat—was go ghost hunting!

zoegirl: no way

mad maddie: way! there's a building on campus that's supposedly haunted, and my suitemates and I snuck in thru the window and went down to the basement, which is the most haunted part of the entire haunted building.

zoegirl: eek, I would have been worried about the campus police.

zoegirl: was it creepy?

mad maddie: so creepy I can't even tell you. human sacrifice, dogs and cats living together . . . mass hysteria!

zoegirl: haha

mad maddie: ok, but there WAS a spine-tingliness to it all. it was dark and my flashlight went out, and at one point we heard this loud BUMP. we all froze in our tracks and Nekkid Neesa's eyes got huge and she put her finger to her lips.

mad maddie: then, and this part's hilarious, she whispered, "Listen! I smell something!"

zoegirl: ???

zoegirl: why hilarious?

mad maddie: really? I have to explain it to you?

mad maddie: the reason it's funny is cuz you can't hear a *smell*.

zoegirl: ohhhhh

mad maddie: everyone cracked up, but I dunno, maybe you had to be there.

zoegirl: did you actually smell anything?

mad maddie: mildew. cold rock. normal basement smells. except . . .

zoegirl: what?

mad maddie: I did catch a whiff of something hard to

describe. like snot mixed with a wet springer spaniel?

zoegirl: ah. yum. ghost dog?

mad maddie: that's really the only explanation, right? woof!

Tues, Oct 15, 3:00 PM E.D.T.

SnowAngel: peeps! I get my owwie foot checked today, and if it's healed enough, I get to say adios to my crutches. cross yr fingers for me—and yr toes!

Wed, Oct 16, 9:33 AM P.D.T.

mad maddie: good morning, sunshine! ☀

mad maddie: u still wearing yr hospital socks?

SnowAngel: health clinic socks, not hospital socks. get it right, geez!

SnowAngel: but I can wiggle my toes! and I don't have to wrap my foot anymore!

SnowAngel: I have graduated to two large Band-Aids, one on the top of my foot and one on the bottom.

mad maddie: does it hurt?

SnowAngel: a little. sometimes a lot. it's worth it to be almost back to normal—except for the VERY sad part, which is that the doc said no 👠s. boo!!!!

mad maddie: poor Angela. will the agony ever end?

SnowAngel: I know, right?

SnowAngel: I have a scar, tho. it's pretty awesome.

mad maddie: is there a scab? will you save it for me? nom nom nom.

SnowAngel: ermagawd, eating scabs is SO second grade.

SnowAngel: the cook at the Zeta house got fired, tho

mad maddie: scabs . . . second grade . . . sorority house cook . . .

mad maddie: ok, I'll bite. (HA!)

mad maddie: why?

SnowAngel: cuz the food was TOO GOOD, which sucks for those of us who actually like to eat. the next cook will serve only carrots and watercress if the bulimia sisters have anything to do with it.

mad maddie: I really hope you're kidding

SnowAngel: I really wish I were

SnowAngel: do you think there's a difference b/w real bulimia and skinny girl mob mentality? there's this one girl who thinks she's fat because she wears size 23 jeans. size 23! that is TINY!

mad maddie: that's fucked up, bro

SnowAngel: don't even get me started, BRO

SnowAngel: and here's another story for ya. Victoria, a Zeta whose Louis Vuitton clutch I covet, asked my friend Anna and me to give some high school girls a tour of the campus.

SnowAngel: (they were daughters of Zeta alums who are considering coming to UGA, that's why)

SnowAngel: we showed them around, blabbity blah, and along the way, we walked down fraternity row. and guys from different houses started calling out things like "fresh meat" and "looking good, girls" and "come shake your moneymakers for us." stuff like that.

mad maddie: ugh

SnowAngel: I told the high school girls to ignore them, cuz if we responded, it would just encourage them.

mad maddie: SO not my world (thank god)

SnowAngel: then, two seconds after I gave that speech, a Delta Sig called out, "Yo! Angela! Where's my kiss, bitch?" and totally on autopilot, I said, "Brian! Hi!" and ran over to chat with him.

mad maddie: headbang headbang headbang
mad maddie: did you kiss him?

SnowAngel:	no!
SnowAngel:	but Anna *totally* gave me hell for going against my own advice. it was funny.
mad maddie:	**good for Anna. I like Anna.**
SnowAngel:	uh-huh. that's why I'm on the fence about whether to depledge or not. I JUST CAN'T DECIDE.
SnowAngel:	like, I've met some super-nice girls, esp Anna, and I love the times when a bunch of us get together and paint each other's nails and eat popcorn and just hang out. I have fun at the mixers too.
mad maddie:	**that sorority leader girl called u a twat, Angela.**
SnowAngel:	and a fucking diaper-wearing baby
mad maddie:	**wha . . . ? you didn't tell me the diaper-wearing-baby one**
SnowAngel:	a *fucking* diaper-wearing baby. get it right. god.
mad maddie:	**hey, I know. you shld depledge and move to Santa Cruz and be with me. I wld even paint yr nails.**
SnowAngel:	*pinches Maddie's cheeks*
SnowAngel:	awww, sweet Maddie. if only! 😜

Wed, Oct 16, 10:00 AM P.D.T.

mad maddie:	**ooo, wait! what's the latest on Lucy what's-her-face? yr roomie?**
mad maddie:	**is she still stealing Q-tips and raisins? have u reported her to campus police?**
mad maddie:	**An-ge-la!!!!**
mad maddie:	**seriously? yr gone? where did u go and why aren't u coming back?**
mad maddie:	**grrr. curse yr oily hide!**

Thu, Oct 17, 12:42 PM E.D.T.

| zoegirl: | I got an app for my phone called MapMyRun that tells you how far you go, and today I ran two miles! |

SnowAngel:	Zo, that's awesome!
zoegirl:	for any real runner, two miles would be nothing. but thx, cuz for me, the actual running part still sucks and I *always* want to stop two minutes into it.
zoegirl:	but I tell myself, "you can do hard things. you can persevere." and then I think about Doug, and how hard it is to go on without him, and I tell myself I can do that too.
SnowAngel:	have you talked to Doug since yr breakup?
zoegirl:	I've almost called him tons of times, but no.
zoegirl:	I check his FB status all the time, and I send evil thoughts toward Canyon, and I still miss him so much. but I have to move through it, right?
SnowAngel:	oh, sweetie. sounds so hard.
SnowAngel:	yes, you have to move thru it, and yes, you WILL move thru it.
zoegirl:	will I?
SnowAngel:	ooo, I want that girl's boots.
zoegirl:	huh?
SnowAngel:	sorry! I'm on the quad and a girl just walked by wearing the most fabulous brown boots I've ever seen.
SnowAngel:	my brown boots are too big at the top and I have to wear thick socks to fill in the gap. this girl's boots looked like they fit tightly around her calves.
SnowAngel:	it wld be awesome to have a pair of tall boots that actually FIT. 👢
zoegirl:	well. good luck with that.
zoegirl:	also, yesterday Holly and I signed up to be volunteers at a Special Olympics competition that's coming up, and after that we went to dinner together, and after that . . . we kind of kissed.
SnowAngel:	EX-FUCKING-SCUSE ME?

SnowAngel:	did you just say what I think you did? YOU AND HOLLY KISSED?!!!!
zoegirl:	kind of. yeah.
SnowAngel:	holy. fucking. shizz. nickels! Zoe!!!
zoegirl:	you're making a big deal out of it. I don't want you to make a big deal out of it.
SnowAngel:	oh, right, sure, cuz it's noooo big deal at all. are you . . . are you two . . . are you two an item???
zoegirl:	ha. no.
SnowAngel:	but you like her.
zoegirl:	of course I like her. the kiss was more . . . why not, you know?
SnowAngel:	um, NO.
zoegirl:	the subject came up—girls with girls, guys with guys—and Holly said she was pretty much straight-up hetero, but that she did wonder what it would be like to kiss a girl. I thought about it and realized that I was curious too. or at least not uncurious.
SnowAngel:	whoa. so you just . . . kissed her? pucker up, sweetie, smoochie-smoochie?
zoegirl:	it was more of a 3-2-1 thing—not that we had an actual countdown. we just looked at each other, and agreed with our eyes, and did it.
SnowAngel:	fucking fucking shizz nickels. HEAD IS SPINNING. college girl experimentation! yah!
SnowAngel:	what was it like?
zoegirl:	nice. soft. weird and a little embarrassing. lots of things!
SnowAngel:	are you going to kiss her again?
zoegirl:	doubt it—but I'm proud of myself for going for it.
zoegirl:	for being NOT Zoe for that one moment.
SnowAngel:	I disagree. you were still being *you*. you decided to be a you who kissed a girl, that's all, and I think it's totally cool. you were yoloing, baby!

zoegirl:	hmm. maybe.
SnowAngel:	you know it's true.
zoegirl:	what do you think Doug would say?
SnowAngel:	I think he'd say, "holy shizz nickels, my hot ex-girlfriend is so hot for kissing her hot new friend," and then he'd want to shoot himself for letting you go.
zoegirl:	good—that's what I wanted to hear! 😊

Fri, Oct 18, 5:07 PM P.D.T.

mad maddie:	and here it is, Friday night again.
mad maddie:	what is my little filly up to this evening?
SnowAngel:	*looks around* am I yr little filly?
mad maddie:	yes, duh, and what are you doing that makes it impossible to answer yr damn phone?
SnowAngel:	oh. Anna and I were having pre-party shots, and I didn't wanna be rude.
mad maddie:	answering yr phone is rude but txting isn't?
SnowAngel:	yup
SnowAngel:	also we're at the Lambda Chi house now, only Anna's gone off to find a bathroom, which means she cld be gone for hours. bathroom lines at these parties are wretched.
mad maddie:	you're at a frat party? I thought you were gonna depledge.
SnowAngel:	I never said that
SnowAngel:	OH! BUT I HAVE A FUNNY AUTOCORRECT STORY TO TELL YOU!
mad maddie:	ok, tell
SnowAngel:	Reid wanted me to hang out with him tonight instead of going to the Lambda Chi mixer, and I was like, "um, no, parties r fun and there will prolly be dancing."
SnowAngel:	plus I don't want to lead him on.
mad maddie:	cldn't he go to the party with you?

SnowAngel:	not exactly. BUT ANYWAY, I told him no, I can't hang out tonight, but how about we meet for lunch?
SnowAngel:	(this convo happened earlier in the day, btw)
mad maddie:	**ahhhh**
SnowAngel:	he said, "sure, when?" and I said, "awesome, I'll meet you at Shakes Alive in two boners."
mad maddie:	**two boners? hahahahaha. LOVE.**
SnowAngel:	how did hours become boners???
mad maddie:	**I'm just glad yr not leading him on by talking about his big ol' boner. wait—his bonerS, plural.**
SnowAngel:	yadda yadda yadda
SnowAngel:	so that's me, drinking and dancing the night away. you?
mad maddie:	**gonna Skype with Ian in about a boner**
mad maddie:	***hour—damn!**
SnowAngel:	very funny
mad maddie:	**I know, right?**
mad maddie:	**and after that . . . I dunno**
SnowAngel:	you have to do something. it's Friday night.
mad maddie:	**yes, mom. thank you, mom.**
mad maddie:	**I guess Ian and I cld have phone sex and send each other naked pictures . . .**
SnowAngel:	Madigan Kinnick!!!! 💀
mad maddie:	**kidding!**
mad maddie:	**I can't wait for Thanksgiving, tho. I sure miss the guy.**
SnowAngel:	aw, Mads
mad maddie:	**and you and Zoe, obviously.**
SnowAngel:	and we miss you. and Thanksgiving isn't even that far off, praise Bob.
SnowAngel:	but tonight is Friday night. chat with Ian and then go be crazy!

mad maddie: **Zo! that little dude is totes adorbs, as Angela wld say.**

zoegirl: from Instagram? that's Fernando. he's on the Special Olympics team I'm coaching.

mad maddie: **I know. *taps noggin* I read the caption, toots.**

mad maddie: **what's Fernando's event? how old is he?**

zoegirl: ten, and he's doing wheelchair rugby, and it's INTENSE. these kids in their wheelchairs are fast!

zoegirl: they wheel themselves super-fast across the court, and sometimes they ram into each other. sometimes their wheelchairs tip over.

mad maddie: **owwie. when their wheelchairs tip over, do they fall out?**

zoegirl: no, because they're strapped in, so they have to sit there—well, lie there—until a coach or ref runs over and gets them upright.

mad maddie: **Jesus**

zoegirl: I know, but everyone cheers for the kid when he or she goes back into the game, because the point is NOT to feel sorry for them.

zoegirl: talk about yolo, right?

zoegirl: imagine being in a car accident and damaging your spine and never being able to walk again. that's what happened to Fernando. but Mads, he is absolutely living life to the fullest. it's so inspiring.

mad maddie: **cool. kinda makes me feel like there's nothing I shld ever complain about.**

zoegirl: me too

zoegirl: but for the record, Fernando's not a saint or anything. another kid poured a slushie over his head, so he retaliated by pouring a slushie over that kid's head.

mad maddie: **ha—that's funny**

mad maddie: **so the girl you have yr arm around. is that Holly?**

zoegirl: yup. she and I are going to a party tonight, and Gannon's going to meet us there. it'll be my first Big College Party.

mad maddie: **eek!**

zoegirl: I know you're teasing me, but yes! eek! I suck at parties!

mad maddie: **ah, you'll be fine as long as you keep in mind this bit of wisdom, courtesy of "The Onion":**

mad maddie: **"Be open to meeting people, as the friends you make freshman year are likely to be the friends you have throughout college, then fall out of touch with after graduation, then see every three to seven years after that."**

zoegirl: k, great. thanks, Mads.

mad maddie: **u betcha. 👍**

Sun, Oct 20, 9:02 AM E.D.T.

zoegirl: omigod. so THAT'S what a college party is.

zoegirl: hahahahahahaha!

zoegirl: everyone got drunk, even me, and I kissed Holly again, and also Gannon, and yes I feel a little embarrassed thinking back on it all, but at the same time I don't.

zoegirl: I had fun. everyone had fun.

zoegirl: and then—ha again!—the campus police showed up cuz apparently we were making too much noise!

zoegirl: I, of course, had a panic attack and imagined myself getting kicked out of school, going to jail, having a criminal record, and having to explain,

	five years later at a job interview, why I checked "yes" on the application where it says, "Have you ever been convicted of a crime?"
zoegirl:	all of that ran through my head in, like, three seconds.
zoegirl:	but, long story short, Holly was her charming self and told the two police guys that we were playing "Would You Rather" and asked if they wanted to play too. they didn't, but they didn't arrest us, either. or write us up or whatever.
zoegirl:	everyone had to pour out their beer, and the police officers gave us a lecture about underage drinking, but that's all.
zoegirl:	so I've officially gone to my first college party *and* I've officially gotten busted at my first college party.
zoegirl:	yes, I am just that cool. 🍻

Sun, Oct 20, 11:10 AM E.D.T.

SnowAngel:	first of all, I cld not be prouder. you are such a badass!
zoegirl:	I know, right? and . . . hi!
SnowAngel:	and second of all, which WLD u rather?
zoegirl:	???
SnowAngel:	kiss Holly or Gannon? 😜
SnowAngel:	I can't believe my little girl had a threesome!
zoegirl:	it was not a threesome. we were just goofing around.
zoegirl:	AND we said out loud that we were just goofing around and that none of us wanted it to be anything more than that.
zoegirl:	it was an experiment. do you have a problem with that?
SnowAngel:	I dunno. kissing a girl once I can write off as an

	experiment. kissing a girl TWICE, and we might be looking at Zoe gone wild.
zoegirl:	nope, not wild.
zoegirl:	well, maybe a little wild . . .
SnowAngel:	for real: do you like Holly as in *like* like her? you know I'm totally cool with it if you do.
zoegirl:	yes, Angela, I know. but I don't.
SnowAngel:	cuz I wld love you no matter what. just sayin'.
SnowAngel:	did you use tongues?
zoegirl:	omg. Holly is awesome and so is Gannon, but we're all just buds. the kissing thing . . . just happened.
zoegirl:	AND you've kissed random people at parties too, if I remember correctly.
SnowAngel:	a) RANDOM and b) guys, not "people." Holly and Gannon aren't random and HOLLY IS A GIRL.
zoegirl:	you're so funny. would a girl kissing a girl really be a big deal at UGA? at Kenyon, everyone is way more relaxed about stuff like that.
SnowAngel:	huh
zoegirl:	yup. but the best thing about last night?
zoegirl:	I didn't think about Doug once. 😄

Sun, Oct 20, 3:30 PM P.D.T.

mad maddie:	**I just ate an entire bag of M&M's. an entire ONE POUND bag of M&M's.**
SnowAngel:	that's a lot of M&M's
SnowAngel:	*I* just bought a pair of Aquatalia boots on Zappos, except not really cuz I am poor. but I want to. Zappos is SO ADDICTIVE!
mad maddie:	**so are M&M's. I feel kinda sick.**
SnowAngel:	the boots I want are kinda like the boots I saw a girl wearing a few days ago. they're tall and brown and gorgeous.
mad maddie:	**don't you already have a pair of tall brown boots?**

SnowAngel:	but these are skinny-around-the-calf boots! and if I buy them, I'll never need another pair of boots again! do you know how many years I've spent searching for skinny boots???
mad maddie:	**zero?**
SnowAngel:	my whole life I've been searching! and what if they never make them again? what if this is my only chance?
SnowAngel:	I think I'll have nightmares if I don't order them. I really do. if there's one thing I've learned in my business class, it's that if resources are scarce, demand will be high.
mad maddie:	**OMIGOD YR RIGHT ORDER THEM THIS INSTANT U FOOL!**
SnowAngel:	*huffs*
SnowAngel:	now you're just teasing me. 😊
mad maddie:	**me? teasing YOU? no way. plus, those words you used—scarce and resources, etc. etc.—make me think you've learned more than that one thing in your biz class, girlie.**
SnowAngel:	hmmm
SnowAngel:	why yes! I have! quel surprise!
SnowAngel:	quel surprise number deux: YOU ACTUALLY DISCUSSED MY BOOT OBSESSION WITH ME. holy fudge nuts, what is the world coming to?
mad maddie:	**cuz I ♥ you. and I secretly ♥ boots, and discussing boots, and I cld spend my whole day chatting about boots. really.**
SnowAngel:	weirdo potato. go to the boots section on Zappos! you will be hooked!

Mon, Oct 21, 6:55 PM E.D.T.

zoegirl:	so. Doug's Facebook status. did you see?
SnowAngel:	I did. *winces*

SnowAngel:	is that Canyon in the picture? 😟
zoegirl:	the girl he's got his arm around? that would be Canyon, yes.
zoegirl:	it made my heart literally stop when I first saw it, but then I shut my laptop, put on my running shoes, and went for a run. three miles today, baby!
SnowAngel:	yr awesome.
SnowAngel:	but you know, that picture doesn't necessarily mean anything. well, it means Doug and Canyon are friends, but it doesn't mean they're lovers.
zoegirl:	no, they're together, because Doug told me. he sent me a message saying he wanted me to hear it from him first, but he sent the message AFTER posting the pic. I know because of the time stamp.
zoegirl:	but who cares, right?
SnowAngel:	not you! hell no!
zoegirl:	except I do, obviously
SnowAngel:	I know. I wld too. anyone wld. 😞
SnowAngel:	ooo—you should send him back a message that says, "oh, no big, I'm a kissing fool these days anyway."
zoegirl:	yeahhhhh. no.
zoegirl:	but at dinner I told Gannon and Holly about Doug, and that led to them talking about their high school girlfriends/boyfriends, and that led to a whole conversation about sex and relationships and why we're attracted to certain people and not others.
zoegirl:	for example, Gannon ONLY likes big girls, or so he claims.
SnowAngel:	big as in chubby? big as in fat?
zoegirl:	big as in big. I didn't press him for specifics.

SnowAngel:	but he kissed you and you are NOT big.
zoegirl:	yes, but our kissing wasn't real, as I have told you many times. or, real but not romantic in any way.
SnowAngel:	I think it's good that Gannon likes big girls. we're brought up to believe that a girl CAN'T BE FAT OR SHE WILL DIE, but that's not true, so good for Gannon.
zoegirl:	I agree
SnowAngel:	what about Holly? what's her type?
zoegirl:	guys over girls, but I've already told you that. slender, muscular, and preferably taller than she is. a soccer player's build, basically.
zoegirl:	oh, and smart. not being smart is a deal breaker.
zoegirl:	Holly's roommate, on the other hand, only dates black guys.
SnowAngel:	why only black guys? is she black? (and am I being racist by asking? I honestly don't know. I think things ARE different at UGA than at Kenyon!)
zoegirl:	she's white. her name's Jessica, and according to Holly, she's sworn off dating any white guys because the chemistry is never there.
SnowAngel:	but it's there with black guys?
zoegirl:	apparently
SnowAngel:	huh
SnowAngel:	what did you tell them your type was?
zoegirl:	I told them I didn't know, which is true.
zoegirl:	I thought my type was Doug, but Doug isn't a type. he's just . . . Doug.
SnowAngel:	well, maybe you don't have to have a "type." there are lots of 🐟 in the sea and lots of types of 🐟 too.
zoegirl:	I agree. I asked Holly if she would consider dating

a big hairy football player, and she was like, "no thank you." but then she thought about it and said, "Unless there was a spark between us. In that case, I might."

SnowAngel: hmm. it all comes down to the mysterious spark, doesn't it? 🔥

Tues, Oct 22, 12:00 PM E.D.T.

SnowAngel: o.m.g.

SnowAngel: I have two HUGELY shocking things to tell y'all. which do you want to hear first?

mad maddie: is that a rhetorical question?

SnowAngel: is what a rhetorical question?

SnowAngel: no, nvm. I don't even know what a rhetorical question is. I never have, and when ppl use that phrase, I just nod and look wise.

mad maddie: in that case, I choose Thing One. Zo?

zoegirl: 👍

zoegirl: but I'm supposed to be doing a makeup lab, so if I suddenly disappear, that's why.

SnowAngel: Thing One it is. I made the foolish decision to step on a scale in the Zeta house . . .

mad maddie: scales r for wimps

SnowAngel: AND I HAVE GAINED THE FRESHMAN FIFTEEN. AAAAGHHHHH.

SnowAngel: I shld have known, cuz all my jeans have gotten tight, but I thought, ya know . . . well, I don't know what I thought.

mad maddie: does that mean u have a muffin top? muffin tops are smexy.

SnowAngel: heyyyyy! you told me to never use that word!

mad maddie: muffin? oh, sorry.

SnowAngel: *gives Maddie evil eye*

zoegirl: I am sure you look fabulous and lush and curvy,

	Angela. and now you're my friend Gannon's type! which is awesome, because Gannon rocks!
SnowAngel:	which is NOT awesome, cuz Gannon is in Ohio and I am in Athens, and are you saying I'm now a "big girl"??!
zoegirl:	I've actually lost weight since starting college, probably because of running.
zoegirl:	I'm down to 109 lbs. I haven't weighed 109 lbs since sophomore year of high school.
SnowAngel:	*glowers*
SnowAngel:	thx. so helpful.
zoegirl:	it means I can't donate blood anymore, because you have to be 110 lbs or more to donate blood.
mad maddie:	**well that must cramp your style.**
mad maddie:	**does somebody want your blood? is this actually a problem?**
zoegirl:	IF the opportunity came up, that's all I'm saying.
mad maddie:	**109 lbs is measly, and Angela, I've ballooned up to 200 pounds, so don't even worry.**
SnowAngel:	you do not weigh 200 lbs, you big liar.
mad maddie:	**big is right. *pats tummy* I'm proud of my tub!**
SnowAngel:	I am NOT proud of my tub, and I want it to go away, but the thought of making it go away is horribly depressing. I DO NOT DO WELL WITH SELF-DEPRIVATION!
mad maddie:	**which is why *I* say . . . if ya want it, eat it. or wear it as a hat.**
zoegirl:	Maddie, you are so random.
zoegirl:	Angela. if you gained any weight, it's because you've been on crutches, you goof. now that you're not, you'll go back to being more active and everything will even out. don't worry.
SnowAngel:	will it, tho? will it?
SnowAngel:	cuz I've also been drinking a ton more than I ever

	have. a cup of beer is 150 calories! lots of beer = lots of calories!!!
mad maddie:	so stop drinking beer
SnowAngel:	but then I will be BORING ANGELA, and the mean girl in my sorority will yell at me for being lame!
mad maddie:	and I quote from the Bible: thou shalt not let a sorority girl named Candy dictate anything about your personal lifestyle, or thou shalt turn into a pillar of salt.
SnowAngel:	TANDY. not candy.
mad maddie:	mmm . . . candy . . . 🍭 🍬 🍬
SnowAngel:	all right, we are moving on to Thing Two, cuz y'all are SO not helping.
mad maddie:	whatever. we love u the way you are. right, Zo?
zoegirl:	yes . . . shhh . . . I have to text quietly because TA is here. I am supposed to be doing important science things!
mad maddie:	*exaggerated whisper*
mad maddie:	OK, WE WON'T TELL IF U DON'T
SnowAngel:	Thing Two is that a senior Zeta just sent out an email blast saying that she's fricking getting married.
SnowAngel:	MARRIED! SHE IS 21!
mad maddie:	whoa. is that what sorority girls do, get married their senior year? isn't it called the "M.R.S." degree or something?
SnowAngel:	I am NOT getting married my senior year, I promise you that.
mad maddie:	if you do, can I be a bridesmaid? will you be embarrassed to have a 200 lb bridesmaid in your entourage?
SnowAngel:	😦
SnowAngel:	my inner critic is very loud today, so I wld appreciate a little kindness.
mad maddie:	hey, I'm making fun of ME, not you. I've seen the

pics you've posted, and if you really have put on 15 lbs, which I doubt, it sure doesn't show. right, Zo?

mad maddie: **Zo???**

SnowAngel: see? she doesn't agree!

mad maddie: **no, she's just off doing Important Science Things.**

mad maddie: **believe what you want, Angela, but you are one sexy tamale.**

Tues, Oct 22, 3:34 PM E.D.T.

SnowAngel: oh! meant to tell y'all: I've been checking Jana's Twitter feed every so often, and her FB, and, dudes . . .

SnowAngel: this is going to sound mean, and maybe it is, but she's put on *more* than fifteen pounds, and from the looks of it, the extra weight all ended up on her face.

SnowAngel: she's like . . . round. like she got stung by a bee. LOTS of bees.

SnowAngel: I can't even make fun of her cuz I feel sorry for her. remember in high school how we said that one day she'd have no friends cuz she's so awful and treats ppl so badly?

SnowAngel: I wonder if that's happened now that she's at college without her posse. like, maybe she's eating out of loneliness?

SnowAngel: her tweets are weird too.

SnowAngel: like one was "bring out your dead." what the . . . ?
😑

SnowAngel: another was "I almost cut myself today," with a pic of the underside of her arm.

SnowAngel: I guess it's a Halloween thing, but it's dumb and creepy and . . . and NEEDY. like she wants everyone to feel sorry for her cuz she "almost" cut herself.

SnowAngel:	I mean, maybe she was saying, "oops, I was slicing a bagel and I almost cut myself by accident," but it didn't seem like it, cuz she attached a pic of the underside of her arm.
SnowAngel:	*shakes it off*
SnowAngel:	anyway . . . I'm so glad I have both of you. that's all.

❤ ❤ ❤

Wed, Oct 23, 4:15 PM E.D.T.

zoegirl:	we're having our last Special Olympics walk-through before the competition on Saturday. the kids are soooo cute.
mad maddie:	walk-through or wheel-through? as in WHEELchairs. get it? get it?
zoegirl:	*disapproving stare*
mad maddie:	oh, plz. was funny.
mad maddie:	if I were in a wheelchair, I'd want ppl to make jokes (if they were funny). I'd wanna be treated the same as anyone else, not as if I were some fragile flower.
zoegirl:	but they're not all in wheelchairs. some are on crutches, some are amputees, some have prostheses.
mad maddie:	when you say "amputee," does that mean that some of them are missing a leg? yikes. on the day of the competition, I sure hope they don't get off on the wrong foot!
zoegirl:	Maddie!
mad maddie:	if you can't laugh, you might as well be dead.
zoegirl:	why are we talking about this? how did this happen?
mad maddie:	because you want to feel sorry for mopey ppl. I want to tell mopers to STOP being sad, cuz what good does it do?

mad maddie: if I'm feeling depressed, I say, "oh, shut up, self. it's not like you lost a leg, so quit yer whining and grow up, loser."

zoegirl: but you're not a loser

zoegirl: and Mads, are you feeling depressed?

mad maddie: no

zoegirl: then why did you say that?

mad maddie: dude, I say all sorts of things. and yes, I sometimes wonder if life has any meaning. don't you?

zoegirl: all right, rewind.

zoegirl: but I know what it feels like to be depressed. you can tell me if you are, Mads.

mad maddie: I'm not depressed. I'm just a nihilist. I'm in a what's-the-point mode.

zoegirl: the point is . . .

zoegirl: the point is that life is so beautiful, even with the depressing parts thrown in. if you were here, if you saw these kids zooming around the gym, laughing and grinning and throwing balls at each other, no way would you say you're a nihilist.

mad maddie: all right, I'm not a nihilist. healed!

zoegirl: you're not telling me something. what are you not telling me?

zoegirl: ok, no answer.

zoegirl: do Zara and the Esbees know how you're feeling?

mad maddie: what? no.

mad maddie: they don't even know what the word "nihilist" means.

mad maddie: well, actually I'm pretty sure they do. but they're into DOING stuff, you know? and they're fine with me hanging out with them, but holding my hand and patting my back wldn't exactly be their thing.

zoegirl: but they're your friends! if you're depressed, wouldn't they want to know?

mad maddie: to which I say: SINCE they're my friends, I refuse to bug them with it.

mad maddie: everything is golden, Zoe. seriously. just last night we came THIS CLOSE to flying to Vegas for a midweek let's-be-crazy fling.

zoegirl: you did not

mad maddie: yeah, we actually did. me, Zara, Nekkid Neesa, and this guy Neesa's going out with named Leon.

zoegirl: Maddie, you are full of it. this time you really are making this up, aren't you? to make fun of me?

mad maddie: um, if I wanted to make fun of you—which I don't—I think I'd do it by making fun of you.

mad maddie: you said you're worried I'm depressed. I said I'm not. I'm now giving proof, all right?

zoegirl: you also said you're a nihilist. like, ten seconds ago. and now everything's "golden"?

mad maddie: we rented a Zipcar and Zara drove us to the airport and we got all the way to the ticket counter before Leon remembered that he was terrified of flying. Zara said she'd just give him some anti-anxiety meds, but then she realized she didn't have any.

zoegirl: Maddie?

mad maddie: yes?

zoegirl: nvm. they're calling me over to time the wheelchair race. mwah! 😊

Thu, Oct 24, 2:22 PM P.D.T.

mad maddie: it has not stopped raining since Wednesday. Santa Cruz, you so crazy.

SnowAngel: I thought CA was the Land of Sunshine.

mad maddie: exactamundo. where's my vitamin D?

mad maddie:	**so have you lost that weight yet?**
SnowAngel:	*gives Maddie the finger*
mad maddie:	**ooo, a finger! yay! already got ten of them, tho, so I'm tossing it back atcha.**
SnowAngel:	you, go stand in the corner.
mad maddie:	**what? why? I'm just being a supportive friend by asking how the Fatty Patty problem is going.**
SnowAngel:	stop it, Maddie. yr being mean.
mad maddie:	**omg, I teased Zoe and she got all huffy too. such drama queens.**
SnowAngel:	*gazes at friend reproachfully*
mad maddie:	**fine. I take back the Fatty Patty remark. GEEZ.**
SnowAngel:	I *was* going to tell you something really sweet that Reid did, but I'm no longer in the mood. call me later, when you're back to being yourself!

Thu, Oct 24, 5:40 PM E.D.T.

SnowAngel:	Maddie just called me Fatty Patty. 😟
zoegirl:	are you serious?
zoegirl:	what is going on with her?
SnowAngel:	wish I knew. she blamed it on us, said we're drama queens.
zoegirl:	maybe she's having a bad day. or a bad week. there's something up with her for sure, but every time I try to call her on it, she finds a way to duck the question.
SnowAngel:	if something's wrong, why won't she tell us about it? why won't she let us be a shoulder for her to cry on?
zoegirl:	um, because Maddie doesn't cry?
SnowAngel:	but that's stupid.
SnowAngel:	she prolly thinks she's "being strong." but it doesn't count if it makes her mean.
zoegirl:	she's not truly mean, though. not deep down.
SnowAngel:	whatever

SnowAngel:	wanna hear something super-sweet that Reid did?
zoegirl:	absolutely!
SnowAngel:	he knows I haven't been feeling so great about myself, and UNLIKE Maddie, he wanted to help me feel better. so he came to my room and we watched "Juno" on his laptop. remember that movie?
zoegirl:	about the girl who gets pregnant in high school? I thought it was great, but you said it was too indie for yr taste.
SnowAngel:	did I?
zoegirl:	you also said that looking at the boyfriend character burned your retinas because he was so dorky.
zoegirl:	Michael Cera! yes! I can't believe I called his name up!
SnowAngel:	excuse me, but those track shorts? his skinny pale thighs? that horrible sweatband . . . ?
SnowAngel:	doesn't matter, tho, cuz he was a good guy. somehow I missed that the first time I saw the movie.
zoegirl:	or maybe you've changed since the first time you saw the movie. maybe you've learned that dorky boys—cough cough Reid cough cough—aren't as bad as you thought.
SnowAngel:	for the record, Reid is waaaaay cuter than the Michael Cera character whose name I can't remember.
zoegirl:	oh, is he, now? 😏
SnowAngel:	ignoring!
SnowAngel:	do you remember when Juno asks her dad if love is even possible, and if so, if it can last?
zoegirl:	ha. I've wondered that myself.
SnowAngel:	oh shit, Zoe. *facepalm*
SnowAngel:	was not talking about Doug, I swear. did NOT mean to bring up bad memories.

zoegirl:	I know. it's fine. go on.
SnowAngel:	well, Juno's dad is all grizzled and rough around the edges. NOT touchy-feely at all.
SnowAngel:	but he gives Juno an honest answer. he says, "The best thing you can do is find someone who loves you when you're pretty, when you're ugly, when you're mad, when you're happy. Someone who, no matter what, is still going to think the sun shines out of your ass."
zoegirl:	aw. it's not the way I would have put it, but . . . yeah.
SnowAngel:	and then Reid paused the movie, looked straight at me, and said, "Ok, Angela? Ok?"
zoegirl:	oh my god. was he saying he LOVES you?
SnowAngel:	no!!!!
SnowAngel:	he was saying that fifteen pounds doesn't mean anything. that it doesn't change who I really am.
zoegirl:	he was saying more than that, Angela. and he has excellent taste. you're awesome.
SnowAngel:	*plugs ears* la la la can't hear u la la la
zoegirl:	do you like him back? I'm not suggesting you're in love with him, but you talk about him A LOT. to me it seems like you think of him as more than just a friend.
SnowAngel:	Zoe, some of my Zeta sisters saw Reid and me at Shakes Alive. they saw Reid, they looked at Reid, and then they looked very deliberately at me. they made it clear, the next time I was at the Zeta house, that Reid was not boyfriend material.
zoegirl:	how did they do that?
SnowAngel:	by saying, and I quote, "Angie, darlin', your friend is a doll, but you do know that he's not boyfriend material for an Alpha Zeta . . ."
SnowAngel:	pretty hard to misinterpret, wldn't you say?

zoegirl:	but . . . ick! that is wrong on so many levels!
SnowAngel:	*shrugs*
zoegirl:	do they really call you Angie?
SnowAngel:	sometimes
zoegirl:	do they really call you darlin'???
SnowAngel:	darlin' or slut, depending on the situation.
SnowAngel:	but not just me. everyone's either a darling or a slut.
zoegirl:	BUT ANGELA. you wouldn't honestly let your sorority sisters, or anyone else, tell you who you could go out with, would you?
zoegirl:	and *do* you like Reid in the going-out-with way???
SnowAngel:	argggh
SnowAngel:	he's my best UGA friend, other than Anna. we see each other every day. he makes me laugh, and he cheers me up when I'm feeling down.
zoegirl:	he goes on late-night donut runs for you . . .
SnowAngel:	he goes on late-night donut runs for me . . .
	🍩 🍩 🍩
SnowAngel:	but do I *like* him like him?
SnowAngel:	😐
zoegirl:	if you can't flat-out say no, that itself says something.
SnowAngel:	sighhhhhhh
zoegirl:	all right, try this. if you were going on a two-day car trip with someone, would you rather go with Reid or your sorority sisters?
SnowAngel:	there are over 300 Zetas, Zoe. 300 Zetas plus me wld not fit in a car.
zoegirl:	hardy hardy har
zoegirl:	in that case, would you rather go on a car trip with Anna or with Reid?
SnowAngel:	where are we going?

SnowAngel:	also, that's not fair. that's asking me to choose b/w two friends, not b/w a friend and a sorority sister.
zoegirl:	**so your sorority sisters aren't your friends . . . ?**
SnowAngel:	*strangles Zoe*
SnowAngel:	enough, you annoying person! you've made your point!
zoegirl:	**good!**
zoegirl:	**what point?**
SnowAngel:	I don't know, except that initiation is in two weeks. that's when I go from being a pledge to being a full-fledged sister, so . . .
SnowAngel:	do I go thru with it or not?
zoegirl:	**God, don't ask me!**

Fri, Oct 25, 4:05 PM E.D.T.

SnowAngel:	omg, you guys. today has been SUCK.
SnowAngel:	showed up for pledge meeting with my hair in a ponytail and was told I looked like hell.
SnowAngel:	so I returned to dorm room to fix hair before going to frat party tonight, and guess what?
SnowAngel:	Lucy! at my bureau, with A BLOB OF MY PHILOSOPHY HOPE IN A JAR MOISTURIZER IN A DIXIE CUP!
SnowAngel:	I was like, "Lucy???"
SnowAngel:	and then she squealed and dropped the dixie cup, meaning that my Hope in a Jar was now "hope splattered on gross dorm room floor."
SnowAngel:	"LUCY?!!!" I said again, very sternly. "wld you care to explain?"
SnowAngel:	"explain what?" she asked.
SnowAngel:	"why you're stealing my beauty products!!!!" I yelled. I'm telling you, I wanted to strangle that girl!
SnowAngel:	first she blushed, and then all the color drained out of her face. and then . . . and THEN!
SnowAngel:	"you mean this?" she said, pointing at the floor

where the splattered moisturizer was. "it's not yours. how do you know it's yours?"

SnowAngel: "because it IS," I said.

SnowAngel: "are you sure?" Lucy said. "I mean, you have so much beauty stuff. so many types and kinds of products . . . maybe you're confused."

SnowAngel: and then she gestured at my night cream and my Kate Somerville deep tissue repair cream and the Laura Mercier foundation that I sometimes mix with my moisturizer since it's too thick on its own. also my Tarte maracuja oil, which you KNOW I love, and my cheek color and my lip stain and all my lipglosses and eyeshadows and primers and mascaras and my Shu Uemura eyelash curler and EVERYTHING.

SnowAngel: wtfffffffffffff?

SnowAngel: do I enjoy beauty products? yes.

SnowAngel: do I have so many that I get confused about what's mine and what isn't? hells no! and even if I did, does that give Lucy the right to help herself to whatever she wants?

SnowAngel: not to mention that you CAN'T share mascara or you could get eye diseases, unless that's a myth, but anyway, gross! no thank you, Lucy's eyelashes!

SnowAngel: I told her, calmly, that I was very aware of my beauty product inventory, and that I was not and never wld be confused about such an important topic.

SnowAngel: she said, "why are you yelling?"

SnowAngel: she tried to hide something behind her back, but I wrestled it away, and it was a Ziploc bag full of other tubes and little containers and half a dozen of my individually wrapped facial wipes. I said, "omigod are you a psycho? are you a HOARDER?"

SnowAngel: she said ow and started hunting for a Band-Aid, but I was so not letting her off the hook just because of a little blood.

SnowAngel: "this is MY STUFF, Lucy," I said. "you can't take my stuff without asking."

SnowAngel: "I'm not," she said. her eyes were huge and starting to look teary, which pissed me off even more because it made me feel sorry for her even though she was the psycho hoarder, not me.

SnowAngel: "then who is?" I said. "your invisible friend named Marge?"

SnowAngel: "Marge?" she said, wrinkling her forehead.

SnowAngel: "and what wld happen if I went and searched behind the dumpster, huh?" I said. "wld I discover your stash—I mean Marge's stash—of stolen contraband? HMMMM?"

SnowAngel: I was proud of myself for "contraband," btw. I felt very "Law & Order," and the only thing that ruined it was her stupid trembling lip, because then I felt like a huge jerk. I rubbed my hand over my face and said, "fine. whatever. just . . . leave my stuff alone. I don't mess with YOUR stuff, do I?"

SnowAngel: she said in this tiny voice, "you can if you want to," and suddenly *I* was the big jerk, or that's what it felt like. because she was being so meek and I was being so . . . not.

SnowAngel: I had to get out of there because I didn't know what to think, or what to say, and when you have to escape YOUR OWN ROOM in order to not feel guilty about the fact that yr psycho roommate is messing with your stuff, you know things are bad.

SnowAngel: I didn't even get to do my hair, because my straightening iron is in my room, while I am sitting in the hall with my hair still in a ponytail.

SnowAngel: SHE EVEN SMELLED LIKE LA LA MALIBU, WHICH AS
YOU KNOW IS MY SIGNATURE SCENT!

SnowAngel: she claimed it was an "accident." that it "spilled"
when she was reaching for something else, and that
she actually felt faint because of how strong it was.
OMFG!!!!!!!!!

Fri, Oct 25, 2:47 PM P.D.T.

mad maddie: **are you still locked out of your room, Ms.**
Ponytailed and Pathetic?

SnowAngel: not "locked out." self-exiled.

SnowAngel: and no. I'm now in the convenience store on the
first floor of my dorm, cuz Lucy *also* stole my box of
Kleenex, the good kind with lotion.

SnowAngel: the only Kleenex they sell here is the scratchy
institutional-grade Kleenex that isn't even real
Kleenex. it's called "Dub'l Puff 1-ply Facial Tissue." I
don't even know where to begin.

mad maddie: **I don't either.**

mad maddie: **if it's 1-ply, shldn't it be called Sing'l Puff?**

SnowAngel: I was sitting outside in the hall, but the longer I sat
there, the more worked up I got. finally I told myself,
"Angela, this is stupid. you are allowed to go into
your own room."

mad maddie: **right you are**

SnowAngel: so I did, and I saw that she'd put back my moisturizer
and the tubes of makeup-y stuff. yay, right?

SnowAngel: but nooooo, cuz she rewarded herself for being
so virtuous by stealing my box of Kleenex instead.
throws hands up in air

mad maddie: **what'd you do?**

SnowAngel: I said, "Lucy? why did you take my box of Kleenex?"
and she blinked really fast and said, "what box of
Kleenex?"

SnowAngel: "the yellow box of Kleenex right there," I said, pointing at her man bag, where the corner of my Kleenex box was poking out as clear as day.

SnowAngel: so get this! she zipped her man bag all the way shut, clutched it to her chest, and said, "I think you're confused."

mad maddie: why do you call it her "man bag"? IS it a man bag?

SnowAngel: I said, "hell yeah, I'm confused! two minutes ago my Kleenex box was on my bedside table and now it's in your stupid man bag! and, newsflash, zipping your man bag up doesn't make what's inside of it magically disappear!"

mad maddie: what then? did you march over and say, "unhand your man bag, you cad!"

SnowAngel: no, cuz she stood up and scuttled out of the room like a . . . like a crab. a crab clutching its ugly crab man bag. I yelled, "bring back my Kleenex! give me back my Kleenex!!!"

mad maddie: and yet . . .

mad maddie: it's Dub'l Puff for you now, huh?

SnowAngel: you better not be laughing.

SnowAngel: and if I end up mysteriously dead and chopped into pieces, you have to go to the police with this. promise?

mad maddie: yes ma'am. absolutely.

SnowAngel: in the meantime . . . well, I don't know. Lucy still claims she isn't stealing my stuff, but how she expects me to buy that load of crap is beyond me. I'm going to video her in the act and she WILL get her comeuppance!

Sat, Oct 26, 1:28 PM E.D.T.

SnowAngel: hello, my friends. this is a public service

	announcement to inform you both that Reid and I have planned a stakeout for this afternoon.
SnowAngel:	we have rearranged my room so that there is just enough space, barely, to hide behind my bed.
SnowAngel:	we will be hiding there vair soon, stocked with chips, Coke, and of course our phones. Reid is going to video Lucy. I'll take the still shots.
SnowAngel:	and of course we won't eat the chips once we hear her coming. too loud, der.
SnowAngel:	wish us luck! 🍀

Sat, Oct 26, 1:34 PM E.D.T.

zoegirl:	I'm at Special Olympics competition. is almost time for Fernando's event so can't chat. but Angela! you are crazy! it is impossible to do a stakeout IN A DORM ROOM BEHIND A DORM-ROOM-SIZE BED. I'm going to write a short story about you and your craziness for my creative writing class!

Sat, Oct 26, 1:38 PM E.D.T.

zoegirl:	not your dorm-room-size bed. *facepalm*
zoegirl:	not saying your bed is size of a dorm room (though wld be awesome).
zoegirl:	Angela?

Sat, Oct 26, 1:40 PM E.D.T.

SnowAngel:	it's almost time! we are ensconced behind bed and I hear Lucy chatting with Kristi-who-always-smells-like-curry, which means SHE IS IN THE HALL!
SnowAngel:	also Reid says hi to both of you, but he is a very loud potato chip cruncher and he is going to have to stop that when
SnowAngel:	fuck bye good luck franaodnq!

zoegirl: er, is "franaodnq" supposed to be Fernando?

zoegirl: ok, your ringer's off and you can't text because you're too busy spy-girling. got it.

zoegirl: check in when you can—I'm off to ref wheelchair basketball!

Sat, Oct 26, 11:15 AM P.D.T.

mad maddie: Angela. dude. read yr newsflash.

mad maddie: wiped sleep out of my eyes, peed, brushed away stink breath with minty fresh Colgate, and read yr newsflash again.

mad maddie: then I called u. u did not answer.

mad maddie: then I called Zoe. Zoe *did* answer, but it was loud and basketball-echoey and kids were screaming and cheering. hung up immediately due to too much early-morning stimulation.

mad maddie: are you smushed behind the bed? smothered by potato chip crumbles?

mad maddie: do let us know the status of yr deadness at yr earliest convenience.

mad maddie: sincerely,

mad maddie: me

Sat, Oct 26, 1:23 PM P.D.T.

mad maddie: it has been two hours . . .

Sat, Oct 26, 5:01 PM E.D.T.

zoegirl: Angela, you are in TROUBLE. right, Mads?

mad maddie: hell yeah. *slams fist against open palm* where's the update, fool?

zoegirl: but guess what? Fernando's team won the rugby championship!!!!!!

zoegirl: he was so proud. now his team goes to the

	national competition in DC, and if they win that, they get to go to Australia!
mad maddie:	Australia? fucking AUSTRALIA?
mad maddie:	damn, where do I sign up?
zoegirl:	um, you don't. you are of sound mind and body and not on a Special Olympics team.
zoegirl:	I'm snapchatting you a slideshow of Fernando and his teammates, including a ten-year-old named Kendra who has only one arm but came in second in girls' gymnastics.
zoegirl:	d'ya get?
mad maddie:	awww
mad maddie:	those are both the most inspiring and most heartbreaking pictures I've ever seen.
zoegirl:	no! NOT heartbreaking!
zoegirl:	do you see their smiles, Maddie?
mad maddie:	is Fernando the one in the middle, in the pic where the team's all lined up?
zoegirl:	#42, with "Fernando" printed across the front of his jersey? yep, that's him, genius. 😊
mad maddie:	he does have a great smile. but I can't help it—the pics still make me sad.
zoegirl:	if you were here, you wouldn't feel sad. you'd feel exhilarated.
zoegirl:	you should Google "Special Olympics Santa Cruz." I'm sure there is one, and you could volunteer just like me. 😄
mad maddie:	*grunts*
mad maddie:	*gives Zoe skeptical look*
zoegirl:	why are you being skeptical?
mad maddie:	I'm not. or I was, but not anymore.
mad maddie:	so, u think Angela's alive?
zoegirl:	of course she's alive!

mad maddie: hmm. accusing someone of stealing personal hygiene products, that can ruffle a gal's feathers. Lucy might have brandished a sword and chopped her head off.

zoegirl: I think Reid's cute, from the pics Angela has posted. don't you?

mad maddie: yeah, sure, but I like the dorky genius type.

mad maddie: he's def not frat boy cute.

zoegirl: grrrr. I wish Angela would care less about that and more about other things, like kindness and a sense of humor and being there for her.

mad maddie: her Zeta sisters look like clones.

mad maddie: they all have straight platinum blond hair that hangs to their shoulders, they've all obviously had their teeth whitened, and they all have "admire me/fawn over me" smiles. IS CREEPY.

zoegirl: well, Angela's hair is more strawberry blond than platinum.

mad maddie: but she flat-ironed it to get rid of her waves. in every single picture, she's wearing it straight. what's up with that? is it Zeta Law that you have to have waterfall blond hair?

zoegirl: the black girl doesn't have blond hair.

mad maddie: ohhhh, that's right.

mad maddie: THE BLACK GIRL. the sole black girl in the entire sorority, unless all the rest are hiding.

zoegirl: that is a little weird, I admit

mad maddie: you think?

zoegirl: I secretly hope Angela depledges.

mad maddie: I unsecretly hope she depledges.

zoegirl: I also hope she gives Reid a chance, just to *see* if she likes him as more than a friend.

mad maddie: I'm not holding my breath.

| mad maddie: | hey, congrats to Fernando. tell him I think he rocks. |
| zoegirl: | 👍 |

Sun, Oct 27, 11:28 AM E.D.T.

SnowAngel:	ok ok ok ok ok! before you get all up in my bid'ness, let me just say that yesterday was VERY traumatic as well as DRAMATIC, and sometimes a girl simply cannot be prey to the winds of time.
SnowAngel:	also Halloween is right around the corner, and I was supposed to be at the Zeta house at 3 to help make decorations for the party we're having with the Deltas. (boys! the party is at their frat house, but they expect us to make the decorations. typical!)
SnowAngel:	but then there was the whole hullabaloo with Lucy's phone getting dropped in the toilet, which made me even later, and yeah.
SnowAngel:	the party's going to be great, tho. I found these adorable body part lollipops that look like actual meat!
zoegirl:	body part lollipops? you think I care about body part lollipops for your HALLOWEEN PARTY? why haven't you answered any of my calls?!
SnowAngel:	Zoe! hi!!!!!!!
zoegirl:	Angela! what the hell happened yesterday?
SnowAngel:	have u realized, just as an aside, that you curse now?
zoegirl:	no, I don't.
SnowAngel:	you just said "hell." in high school you wld have said "heck."
zoegirl:	omg. what the heck fucking happened with you and Lucy and Reid yesterday?!!!!!!!!!!
SnowAngel:	relax, relax. that's why I texted, to tell you all about it.
SnowAngel:	it's complicated, tho

zoegirl:	I can handle it.
SnowAngel:	well, to set the scene:
SnowAngel:	there Reid and I were, crouched behind my bed, just chilling with the dust bunnies and our potato chips, chatting and chomping, nom nom nom.
SnowAngel:	then LUCY ARRIVED, and we clamped up those lips of ours PRONTO.
SnowAngel:	(spoiler! there will be unclamping of lips later! but we are not to that part of the story yet!)
zoegirl:	what are you saying? wait—did you and Reid kiss???
SnowAngel:	we clamped our lips
SnowAngel:	we peered oh-so-slyly over the edge of my bed. ◔ ◔
SnowAngel:	AND ALL OF MY SUSPICIONS WERE TRUE! Lucy, not knowing Reid was videoing her every move, sauntered right over to my bureau, just as pretty as u please.
zoegirl:	if I had a roommate? and she—or her boyfriend— secretly videoed me . . . ?
SnowAngel:	Reid's not my boyfriend. sheesh. so off topic.
SnowAngel:	SO, Lucy picked up my much adored Benefit How to Look the Best at Everything kit, unscrewed the tiny tube of concealer, and SNIFFED it!
zoegirl:	eeek. so she really has been going through your stuff.
SnowAngel:	SNIFFING my stuff! and, der! what have I been telling you???
SnowAngel:	she picked up various other moisturizers and lotions, but rejected all of them as well. (which in its own way was quite offensive.)
zoegirl:	omigod. only you.
SnowAngel:	then she found my dry shampoo! the good one from Sephora that smells like grapefruit and actually works!

SnowAngel: AND SHE TOOK IT AND PUT IT IN HER BACKPACK, WHICH MEANS I WAS RIGHT ALL ALONG, AND THAT IS WHEN I SPRANG OUT FROM BEHIND MY BED AND SAID, "AH-HA! YOU *ARE* STEALING MY THINGS! UNHAND MY DRY SHAMPOO, YOU CAD!"

zoegirl: holy cow. did she have a heart attack?

SnowAngel: she jumped a bit, yes. but too bad.

SnowAngel: I said, "and don't go trying to deny it, because my boy Reid here has it all on his phone. he videoed every move you made, and I cld report you to the provost, you know."

SnowAngel: (I don't actually know what a provost is, but I thought it sounded ominously official.)

zoegirl: a provost is second in command to a university's president, basically.

SnowAngel: (really? cool! except I don't actually WANT to know what a provost is . . .)

SnowAngel: "unhand my dry shampoo!" I said.

SnowAngel: "give me yr friend's phone!" she said.

SnowAngel: "what?" I said. "no way. you have to give me my dry shampoo because it is MINE. Reid does NOT have to give u his phone cuz it's HIS. seriously, are you mentally deranged?"

zoegirl: a provost is generally expected to be diplomatic, so you might need to strike that one off your "future jobs" list.

SnowAngel: so Lucy lunged for Reid's phone, which left me no choice but to lunge for *her* phone, which was in her back jeans pocket, which I knew because I saw the lump of it.

zoegirl: why was grabbing Lucy's phone the obvious response to Lucy going after Reid's phone???

SnowAngel: and then there was, u know, a BROUHAHA, and Lucy got all pissed and steam came out of her ears

	because someone accidentally dashed out of the room and down the hall to the bathroom and dropped her phone into the toilet.
zoegirl:	someone, huh?
SnowAngel:	it might have been me.
SnowAngel:	it was me.
SnowAngel:	it happened in the heat of the moment!
SnowAngel:	but don't worry, she retaliated by dropping my dry shampoo into the toilet.
SnowAngel:	flung it, is more like it. and you know what sucks?
zoegirl:	what?
SnowAngel:	her phone didn't end up getting ruined AT ALL, cuz Lucy snatched it out so quickly, and plus I looked up "how to fix a cell phone that's been dropped in the toilet" and found out that if we put it in a bag of dry rice, it wld heal itself.
SnowAngel:	and it did! isn't that cool? the rice sucked up all that toilet water.
SnowAngel:	my dry shampoo, however?
zoegirl:	you can't re-dry dry shampoo once it's gotten wet?
SnowAngel:	that, and even if you cld, who wants to put possibly evaporated, or possibly not, toilet water in her hair?
zoegirl:	how did you get from accidentally flinging Lucy's phone into the toilet to helping her fix it???
SnowAngel:	oh. cuz once all the brawling was over, Lucy told me what was *really* going on, and I totally forgave her, silly.
zoegirl:	I am so confused! what WAS really going on?
SnowAngel:	think about the things she stole: toothpaste, Q-tips, raisins. a comb. dry shampoo. a t-shirt of my dad's that I used as a night shirt until it disappeared. (I figured I'd lost it doing laundry.)
SnowAngel:	what do all those things have in common?

zoegirl:	I have no idea. will you please just tell me?
SnowAngel:	two words: Jermaine. Quenton.
SnowAngel:	I think that's how u spell his last name. maybe Quinton? Quintin?
zoegirl:	Angela . . .
SnowAngel:	ok, ok, he's a homeless man who's been living behind the dumpster behind our dorm. remember when I saw Lucy prowling around that general area?
zoegirl:	was that on the "no more cheese and white bread sandwiches" day?
SnowAngel:	yes! and the reason she was there was cuz she was checking up on Jermaine. in fact, ALL THIS TIME she's been helping him find ways to shower and stay clean and keep the earwax out of his ears.
zoegirl:	and the raisins?
SnowAngel:	snack food!
SnowAngel:	I know what you're thinking. you're thinking, "wldn't it just be easier to sneak food from the cafeteria?"
SnowAngel:	but she wanted to spread around her acts of sneakery, if that makes sense.
zoegirl:	oh, we left the land of making sense loooong ago.
SnowAngel:	and the reason she stole my toiletries was cuz she assumed I had so many I'd never notice.
SnowAngel:	he's really nice. Jermaine, that is. he's just homeless cuz he had a run of bad luck. first he lost his job as a dishwasher, then he fell behind on his rent, then he got evicted from his apartment . . .
SnowAngel:	isn't that awful? that an apartment-owner dude wld kick someone out just cuz he cldn't pay his rent?
SnowAngel:	but now everything's better! cuz Lucy and I are cool with each other, and Jermaine is living with us!
	😃
zoegirl:	EXCUSE ME???

SnowAngel:	I am doing altruism, just like you with the Special Olympics!
zoegirl:	the provost is not going to like this.
SnowAngel:	the provost isn't going to know.
SnowAngel:	anyway, SO glad we got all caught up, but I've gotta run. I'm supposed to be making ghosts out of tissue paper, ya know.
zoegirl:	wait! no! don't you dare tell me a homeless man is living in your dorm room and then run off to make ghosts out of tissue paper!
SnowAngel:	I'm also going to help some of the pledges put their costumes together cuz I'm good at that stuff. tootles 😶

Sun, Oct 27, 12:45 PM E.D.T.

zoegirl:	what about the unclamping of the lips?
zoegirl:	you said that there would be unclamping of lips, but you never got to that part of the story.
zoegirl:	so, this unclamping business
zoegirl:	what, exactly, did your and Reid's unclamped lips *do*?
zoegirl:	you have until this evening to respond. if you don't, I'm turning you in to the provost.

Mon, Oct 28, 4:00 PM E.D.T.

SnowAngel:	Maddie, why did u delete yr Facebook account???
mad maddie:	I dunno. cuz I felt like it, just like you felt like kissing Reid in the hot passionate moment after moving a homeless dude into yr dorm room.
mad maddie:	I had to listen to yr voicemail twenty times to make sure I heard that right, btw.
SnowAngel:	twenty times? 😐
SnowAngel:	liar
mad maddie:	ok, ten times. maybe five.

SnowAngel:	are you trying to change the subject about yr FB?
mad maddie:	**three times. I listened to it three times, all right?**
mad maddie:	**also, I hadn't read the text exchange b/w you and Zoe, so I wasn't caught up in the first place.**
SnowAngel:	you saw texts waiting for you—from ME—and you didn't read them?
mad maddie:	**I was tired. I didn't feel like doing anything.**
SnowAngel:	except delete yr FB account.
SnowAngel:	seriously, why?
mad maddie:	**oh, same reason. tired of dealing with ppl.**
SnowAngel:	I don't understand
mad maddie:	**I never post anything. I hardly read anyone else's posts. so why bother?**
mad maddie:	**in self-defense, I am very good friends with Netflix.**
SnowAngel:	you're tired of "dealing with people." what about yr suitemates? what about Zara and Neesa and the other Esbees?
mad maddie:	**meh**
SnowAngel:	but you have so much fun with them!
SnowAngel:	did y'all have a fight? did something happen?
mad maddie:	**Angela, everything's fine. I'm just not motivated to do much these days.**
SnowAngel:	um, that's NOT fine, Mads. next yr going to tell me that you've moved yr computer into yr closet and soon you'll have no use for the outside world.
SnowAngel:	shld I be worried about you???
SnowAngel:	strike that. I *am* worried about u. Maddie!!! Zoe and I both are!
mad maddie:	**it's a phase. a mid-semester slump.**
mad maddie:	**I miss u guys, ok? and I miss Ian.**
mad maddie:	**I'm just really ready for Thanksgiving.**
SnowAngel:	ah
SnowAngel:	that makes sense. I can't wait for Thanksgiving

either. yay college for having a super-long Thanksgiving break! 🍗 🍻 🍗

mad maddie: agreed

SnowAngel: but until then, will you try to get back into the game?

mad maddie: "get back into the game"?

SnowAngel: dude. don't mock. YOLO, BABY, YOLO!

SnowAngel: that's what you told Zoe when *she* was feeling down.

mad maddie: oh. right.

SnowAngel: do you no longer believe in yolo???

mad maddie: of course I do. can't believe you'd suggest otherwise.

mad maddie: and now back to reality: you kissed Reid???

SnowAngel: aye-yai-yai

SnowAngel: kind of?

mad maddie: was it a GOOD kiss?

SnowAngel: truth?

mad maddie: truth

SnowAngel: it was a scarily excellent kiss, Maddie. as in, there's a very good chance he's the best kisser in the multiverse.

SnowAngel: but it just HAPPENED. and yes, I like him—he's Reid!

SnowAngel: but also, he's . . . Reid. you know?

mad maddie: are you gonna kiss him again?

SnowAngel: dunno. we're going to Shakes Alive for dinner, tho.

mad maddie: I'm going to take that as a yes

mad maddie: if the "but also he's Reid" business has anything to do with your sorority sisters, then screw that. you kissed Reid, not yr sorority sisters. if you start dating him, *you'll* be dating him, not yr sorority sisters.

SnowAngel: yeah, putting that in the Worry About Later file.

SnowAngel: right now I am weighing the merits of wearing a

boob-enhancing bra that feels like a bra and not boobs (as in, sofa-cushion puffy) or a soft lacy bra that does nothing for my booblettes but that makes me feel like a real girl and not a padded girl. thoughts?

mad maddie: **huh. that's a question I've never in my life thought about.**

SnowAngel: cuz u don't have to worry about it. you have tatas galore!

SnowAngel: also, it seems like maybe I'm wired to think about this stuff. not just bras, but clothes and makeup and accessories . . . the whole picture! and I'm good at it, and I'm good at helping other ppl with it, and I think I'm going to make that be my plan for my business class assignment! fashion consultant!

mad maddie: **that's cool, Angela. perfect.**

SnowAngel: isn't it? and I stay after class to talk to my biz prof all the time now, and she's possibly my new hero. SHE MAKES ME THINK, MADDIE. IT IS THE WEIRDEST THING.

mad maddie: **dude. your brain is growing!**

SnowAngel: and yet in the boy department I'm still at a loss. which do you think is more important to a guy: visual or tactile? cleavage or the softness of real boobs?

mad maddie: **go for real. real is better.**

SnowAngel: hmm . . .

SnowAngel: but will any boob-touching actually occur? cuz if not, shldn't I go for the push-up?

mad maddie: **ok, but imagine this: what if no touching occurs tonight, and you go for the push-up, but then the next day, or the next or the next, when touching DOES occur, he's like, "where'd they go?"**

SnowAngel: a) who said there'd be a next and a next, and

SnowAngel: b) I'm not convinced guys are that observant. I mean, if boobs are there, then yes, they observe them. but if it changes to boobs are there being touched, I wonder if maybe the touching takes over . . . ?

mad maddie: **want me to ask Ian?**

SnowAngel: yes, actually! omigod, yes!

SnowAngel: get back to me before six o'clock my time—please???

mad maddie: **I'll do my best.**

Mon, Oct 28, 2:38 PM P.D.T.

mad maddie: **Angela, ya there?**

mad maddie: **Ian says either is fine, but that HE prefers real to padded. but that Reid will be thrilled with any boobage at all.**

mad maddie: **and yes, it was slightly strange to be discussing yr boobs with my boyfriend—but anything for you, hot stuff!** 😛

Tues, Oct 29, 12:03 PM E.D.T.

zoegirl: I'm so happy for Angela and Reid! 🖤 🖤 🖤

mad maddie: **me too, as long as her sorority sisters don't make a voodoo doll of him and stick pins all over it.**

zoegirl: when I talked to her, she finally admitted that she likes him even though she knows the Zetas won't "approve."

mad maddie: **gag gag gag**

zoegirl: I know. but he's her first college boyfriend, and maybe he'll be her first good and true boyfriend, period. I'm *glad* he isn't the sort of guy she'd usually go for. I'm proud of her for branching out. yolo, baby! right?

mad maddie: **maybe we'll get to meet him over Thanksgiving break**

mad maddie: **do you think you'll see Doug over break?**

zoegirl:	I don't know. I doubt I'll make plans to see him, but maybe if someone has a party or something.
mad maddie:	**wld running into him be good, bad, or weird?**
zoegirl:	agh. makes my stomach twist.
zoegirl:	but—and this is crazy liberating—I know I'll be able to handle it either way.
zoegirl:	I feel . . . bigger since being at college. not literally, but in my mind. like I can see more possibilities now. like, I've handled some hard things, but I came out on the other side, and I'm ok. I'm still me.
zoegirl:	if anything, I'm MORE me. it feels good. 😊

Wed, Oct 30, 5:00 PM P.D.T.

mad maddie:	**I got yr voicemail, Angela, and no, Jermaine cannot sleep on the floor of your dorm room for the rest of the semester.**
mad maddie:	**in fact you shldn't have let him sleep there even for a night and YOU KNOW IT.**
mad maddie:	**I'm sure he is nice. I'm sure he is a gem. I am also very glad that you decked him out in a whole new thrift-store wardrobe that gives him "a look of confident sophistication with a twist of humble beginnings."**
mad maddie:	**but if you're not allowed to have pets in yr dorm room, then guess what? pretty dang sure you're not allowed to keep a homeless man in there either.**
mad maddie:	**whoa—that came out wrong.**
mad maddie:	**but if you and Lucy basically moved OUT of yr room so that Jermaine cld move IN, doesn't that give you yr answer right there???**
mad maddie:	**don't get me wrong. I am glad y'all aren't having a threesome! two nineteen-year-old girls sleeping**

in a cramped dorm room with a fifty-year-old man who is a STRANGER is NOT A WISE IDEA!

mad maddie: but babe, find a local homeless shelter or something. there are resources out there, like churches and stuff. try a church!

mad maddie: and finally, NO, YOU SHLD NOT INVITE HIM TO GO TO THE ZETA HALLOWEEN PARTY!!! ARE YOU INSANE?

mad maddie: let us review:

mad maddie: the party is at a frat house. right?

mad maddie: frat boys BEAT UP HOMELESS GUYS. right?

mad maddie: I'm sure not all frat boys do, but really, Angela?

mad maddie: drunk boys + scruffy old toothless dude who, as you yrself said, gives off a "musty" smell despite numerous showers does not = good times and the formation of lifelong friendships.

mad maddie: inviting Jermaine is a kind thought, but no. just . . . no.

mad maddie: also no to being a slutty unicorn.

mad maddie: the one EXCELLENT decision you've made, tho, is to invite Reid to the party even tho he's not a Greek.

mad maddie: well, it's either an excellent decision or a terrible one.

mad maddie: regardless, power to the people!

Wed, Oct 30, 10:17 PM E.D.T.

SnowAngel: Zo-Zo! you still awake?

zoegirl: I'm in bed. was THIS CLOSE to turning off ringer.

SnowAngel: yay that you didn't! hiiiiiiiiii! *waves enthusiastically*

zoegirl: 😴

SnowAngel: I kissed Reid again. it was most excellent. HE is most excellent, and fine, yes, I LIKE THE GUY.

SnowAngel:	can you believe I'm falling for a geek????
zoegirl:	*I'm* a geek, you know.
SnowAngel:	well, but I'm not kissing you. 😜
SnowAngel:	Reid says I have pretty eyes. isn't that sweet?
zoegirl:	you do have pretty eyes. you have pretty everything.
SnowAngel:	awww! that's what Reid says! 😃
SnowAngel:	he also says I make him feel alive. maybe cuz I've got more energy than he does?
zoegirl:	you have more energy than everyone, goof
SnowAngel:	also he laughs at how I talk to EVERYONE, but he says it's cute.
zoegirl:	it is. I can see how Reid—or any guy—would love to be around you. you're smiley and fun and happy. you're awesome.
SnowAngel:	why thank you!
SnowAngel:	so yeah, we had bagels for dinner, Reid and me.
zoegirl:	Reid and I.
SnowAngel:	heh?
zoegirl:	Reid and *I* had bagels. that's how you say it.
SnowAngel:	um, no, it was Reid and ME. how cld Reid have bagels with you when yr not even here?
zoegirl:	I was correcting your
zoegirl:	nvm
SnowAngel:	so, bagels—nom nom nom—and then we talked and talked and talked, and then we kissed and kissed and kissed, and then at the end of the night, he walked me to Anna's dorm room and made sure I got in safely. isn't that gallant?
zoegirl:	you're still sleeping in Anna's room? Angela!
SnowAngel:	some guys wld be all, "oh, why don't you just sleep with me, hubba hubba," but not Reid.
zoegirl:	what does he think of the fact that you've given your own room to a homeless guy?

SnowAngel:	he thinks . . .
SnowAngel:	oh, why dwell on the negative?
SnowAngel:	anyway, it is harder than you think to give Jermaine the boot!
zoegirl:	**why?**
SnowAngel:	he keeps offering to leave or sleep in the hall. but we can't let him sleep in the HALL, obviously.
zoegirl:	**riiiiight. far better to lock him up in yr dorm room.**
SnowAngel:	he's not locked up. geez!
SnowAngel:	he can leave anytime he wants to, as long as we set up a lookout and create a distraction and whisk him out of the building while no one's watching.
SnowAngel:	we're thinking about getting him a wig, Lucy and me.
zoegirl:	**Lucy and *I*.**
SnowAngel:	what??? LUCY AND ME! you are sooo random!
SnowAngel:	it's bringing the two of us closer, tho. after Lucy saw what a good job I did of freshening up Jermaine's image, she let me give her a makeover too.
SnowAngel:	turns out she's super-pretty when she's not skulking around like a toiletries stealer. also I'm going to throw away her overalls when she's not looking.
zoegirl:	**why can't you help Jermaine get set up in a homeless shelter like Maddie suggested?**
SnowAngel:	cuz they're all full.
SnowAngel:	I had no idea homeless shelters were even allowed to be full.
SnowAngel:	you know what's sad?
zoegirl:	**what?**
SnowAngel:	Jermaine used to have a family. he had a wife and kids, and he loved them so much, and he still does, only they didn't stick around once he lost his job.
zoegirl:	**poor guy**

SnowAngel:	yeah, they moved to New Orleans, which is where his wife's family is.
zoegirl:	**why didn't Jermaine go too?**
SnowAngel:	huh
SnowAngel:	that's a good question.
SnowAngel:	but he said something today that will be stuck in my head forever and ever.
SnowAngel:	he told us again that he hadn't chosen this for himself, being homeless, and that ppl fall thru the cracks all the time. that it can happen to *anyone*.
zoegirl:	**do you agree?**
SnowAngel:	I don't know. do you?
zoegirl:	**I get what Jermaine is saying, I think. but at the same time . . .**
zoegirl:	**you and Maddie and I have each other, and we have our families, and I don't think we'd ever fall through the cracks because we wouldn't let each other.**
SnowAngel:	I said something like that to Jermaine, like how I was sorry that his wife had left him, cuz if two ppl really love each other, they shld stick together thru thick and thin.
SnowAngel:	but HE said, "it wld be nice if love were enough. but it's not."
zoegirl:	**oh, so sad!**
zoegirl:	**he's wrong, though. don't you think he's wrong?**
SnowAngel:	you and Doug were absolutely in love, and that love went away . . .
SnowAngel:	I'm not saying that to make you feel bad, either. I want love to be enough. but I don't wanna be all, "well, Jermaine is Jermaine and I am me, and what happened to him wld never happen to me cuz we are sooooooooo different."
zoegirl:	**but you ARE different.**

SnowAngel:	are we? or do I just have the luxury of thinking we are cuz so far I've been so blessed?
zoegirl:	**Angela. you are asking hard questions.**
SnowAngel:	I know! AND IT'S SO UNLIKE ME!
SnowAngel:	but I'm not just going to say, "good-bye, Jermaine. leave now, please." I'm not going to let other ppl tell me who I'm allowed to be nice to and who I'm not.
zoegirl:	**oh, Angela, I'm sorry. that's not what I meant at all. I'm just worried about you!**
SnowAngel:	I didn't mean YOU.
SnowAngel:	and I'm not just talking about Jermaine either. I'm talking about my Zeta sisters, and Reid, and how some of them keep making comments about how Reid isn't good enough for me.
zoegirl:	**now that IS wrong.**
SnowAngel:	our Cross Over ceremony is this coming Sunday. I'm worried.
zoegirl:	**is that when you cross over from being a pledge to officially being a sister?**
SnowAngel:	uh-huh. we all wear white dresses, and there are candles, and it's very solemn. it's when we're formally initiated into the Alpha Zeta sisterhood.
zoegirl:	**so you're going to do it?**
SnowAngel:	I don't know!!!
SnowAngel:	pros: Anna. having fun things to do, fun things that are planned out for me in advance. meeting new people. watching TV in the Zeta house and eating popcorn and feeling like I'm PART of something. the whole idea of, you know, sisterhood. I *like* the idea of sisterhood!
zoegirl:	**yeah, I can see that**
SnowAngel:	also we do community service projects! and that's good, right?

zoegirl:	what community service projects have the Zetas done?
SnowAngel:	um? car wash? in bikinis?
zoegirl:	impressive
zoegirl:	Angela, you do more community service all by yourself than the whole Zeta chapter does, I bet. you do so many kind things just because you're you!
SnowAngel:	aw, thanks! but it's the "all by yourself" part that makes me anxious.
SnowAngel:	if I depledge, what wld happen? wld the Zetas stop talking to me? wld I be lonely? wld I regret it?
SnowAngel:	I kind of haven't gotten to know the girls in my own dorm very well. Lucy and Jermaine, they're basically the only ppl I know. 😫
zoegirl:	ok. and the cons?
zoegirl:	(although if the girls who are supposed to be your "sisters" would stop talking to you just because you depledged, then I'm not sure that's any sort of real sisterhood . . .)
SnowAngel:	sigh. I know, and that's one of the cons—the fact that I don't TOTALLY feel like I am a Zeta.
SnowAngel:	let's see. other cons wld be the chapter meetings, which are mind-numbingly boring, and the focus on always looking perfect. and the hazing, whether it really was hazing or not. like, wld I have to be a part of that next year, with the new pledges?
SnowAngel:	I'm also not a huge fan of the way the frat guys treat us. not ALL of them. but that story, which might have been an urban legend, about frat boys getting girls drunk and having sex with them? it's just so awful!
zoegirl:	I am so with you there. makes me sick.

SnowAngel:	that kind of stuff doesn't happen at UGA, but the frat guys *do* make lewd comments sometimes. they *do* act, like, entitled sometimes. this one guy got mad at Anna when she wldn't fool around with him, for example. it was at a party hosted by one of the fraternities, and the guy was all, "you're getting free beer. what am *I* getting?"
zoegirl:	that just pisses me off, Angela. doesn't it piss you off?
SnowAngel:	yes! THE JERKY FRAT BOYS ARE TOTAL JERKS!
SnowAngel:	but jerky boys are jerky boys whether they're in frats or not. plus, this is UGA, not a smarty-pants liberal school like Kenyon. people here still use "gay" as an insult. can you believe that?
zoegirl:	ugh, and yes, and ugh again. I'm sorry, Angela.
SnowAngel:	so it's just a lot to think about. if I can be me AND be a Zeta, then yay, and yes.
SnowAngel:	but if being part of the Greek system means buying into the hive mentality, then no thank you. I wld like to think for myself, please, and I don't want anyone giving me a hard time for it.
zoegirl:	so . . . ?
SnowAngel:	so here's what I've decided: I'm bringing Reid to the Halloween party at the Delta house, and if any of the Zetas give me a hard time—OR give him a hard time—then that's it. I'm out.
zoegirl:	meaning you'll depledge?
SnowAngel:	yep. because we're all humans and we shld be nice to each other, end of story.
zoegirl:	agreed. and I do hear you about the good parts of being part of a community, etc.
SnowAngel:	thx. I don't think Maddie does.
zoegirl:	well, it's complicated.

zoegirl:	I'm super proud of you for being willing to stand up for Reid, but I hope it doesn't come to that.
SnowAngel:	me too!

Thu, Oct 31, 10:50 AM E.D.T.

SnowAngel:	Happy Halloween, darlings!!! 🎃
SnowAngel:	I'm dashing to class—class on Halloween? what is wrong with these ppl?—and then with party prep and everything, I'm going to be busy as a 🐝, so I wanted to say "boo" while I cld.
SnowAngel:	BOO!
SnowAngel:	have SO MUCH fun tonight, both of you.
SnowAngel:	Zoe, be bold and look for someone new to have a crush on. it's time. (or just have fun with Holly and Gannon. that's cool too.)
SnowAngel:	and Maddie? no dates with Netflix. NOT ALLOWED, unless you invite a whole bunch of peeps over to watch scary movies.
SnowAngel:	as for me, I'll be terrifying everyone in my sexy princess-of-the-undead outfit. Reid is going as a knight in rusting armor. we will be adorable.
SnowAngel:	I hope and assume that all will go well at the mixer and that it will be la la la, candy and beer and good times.
SnowAngel:	but if it's not . . .
SnowAngel:	if anyone is rude to Reid, then that's it, I'm done, and adios, Zetas.
SnowAngel:	send good thoughts my way! 👿

Thu, Oct 31, 5:45 PM E.D.T.

zoegirl:	hey, Mads. so what *are* you going to do for Halloween?
mad maddie:	hello, Zoe. I have a floppy toenail that is diverting all my attn right now, I'm sorry to say.

zoegirl: oh dear. that gives me a deep sad.

zoegirl: but here's a deep happy: Angela and Lucy got Jermaine hooked up with a Lutheran church, and the church people are going to help him find low-income housing.

zoegirl: she said it was your idea, so yay!

zoegirl: she posted a picture of the three of them on FB, but since you deleted your account . . .

zoegirl: did you get?

mad maddie: whoa

mad maddie: he's, like, a hillbilly. an aging good ol' boy with a scraggly white beard.

mad maddie: for some reason I expected him to be black.

zoegirl: racist

zoegirl: (except I did too, so . . .) 💀

mad maddie: they look happy. true happy, not fake-sorority-smile happy.

zoegirl: I know—and no platinum blond waterfall hair!

zoegirl: but what about you? are you true happy, fake happy, or none of the above?

mad maddie: hmm. a mix?

mad maddie: it's kind of embarrassing to admit, but being thousands of miles away from everyone is harder than I thought.

zoegirl: Maddie! ☹

zoegirl: of course it's hard, and there's nothing embarrassing about saying so. AND PLUS I HAVE KNOWN FOR FIVE THOUSAND YEARS THAT YOU WEREN'T HAVING THE TIME OF YOUR LIFE. so has Angela.

zoegirl: how long have you been feeling this way? cuz you have had *some* good times, right?

mad maddie: yeah, I guess

mad maddie: but Zara and the Esbees . . .

mad maddie:	it's possible they're not as great as I've made them out to be.
zoegirl:	what do you mean?
mad maddie:	they're not awful or anything. they're just . . .
mad maddie:	honestly, they're just not Y'ALL.
mad maddie:	like, a few days ago, Zara made a comment about how her friends were her life, and it was clear she meant her Esbee friends, not me.
zoegirl:	oh, Mads!
mad maddie:	she caught herself right away and said, "my old friends AND my new friends, like you. it's just that I've known Neesa and Taylor and Erica forever. I'd throw myself in front of a train for them, you know?"
mad maddie:	and I do know, cuz I wld totally throw myself in front of a train for you and Angela . . . altho I'd hope it was a Lego train, or a Thomas the Tank Engine train.
zoegirl:	ha
mad maddie:	yeah, see? I can still be funny.
mad maddie:	but for the most part, I feel like I don't know who I am anymore.
mad maddie:	ugh, that sounds so lame. anyway, moping is for wimps, as both you and Angela have pointed out.
zoegirl:	what? neither of us said that!
mad maddie:	anti-yolo, then. same thing.
mad maddie:	as for Zara and my other suitemates, they're fine.
mad maddie:	they're not evil. they're not fabulous. they're fine.
mad maddie:	I decided to stop trying to force it, that's all.
zoegirl:	so . . . you're not going out with them tonight?
mad maddie:	nope
zoegirl:	you're not staying in and doing nothing, though, are you?
mad maddie:	oh plz

mad maddie:	I'm going to the student center to hear a lecture that a famous doctor is giving. the write-up in the school paper said that his grandfather was a true mad scientist whose passion was trying to reanimate the dead, so it's perfect for Halloween.
zoegirl:	cool 👍
mad maddie:	I think so. there'll be slides of corpses and abnormal brains and stuff like that.
mad maddie:	and before you ask, yes, I'm going by myself, but I'm going by myself BY CHOICE.
zoegirl:	isn't there anyone you could invite to go with you? other than Zara and her crowd?
mad maddie:	no. but you don't need to worry, k?
mad maddie:	are you still doing the zombie crawl with Gannon and Holly?
zoegirl:	yeah. I wish you could go with us!!!
mad maddie:	I'll be there in spirit. 👻

Thu, Oct 31, 8:42 PM P.D.T.

mad maddie:	hot tip: yelling at a fire does not make the flames go out.
zoegirl:	huh? what? what fire?
mad maddie:	at the new Taco John's that opened.
mad maddie:	ooo! I never told you, but a new Taco John's opened!
zoegirl:	but then it burned down?
mad maddie:	no, silly. grease fire. someone used a fire extinguisher eventually. this, like, thirteen-year-old kid noticed it first. he stood there pointing and yelling at it.
mad maddie:	"eeeeee!" "eeeeee!" he said.
mad maddie:	afterward he was really embarrassed.
zoegirl:	I hope you comforted him.
mad maddie:	I didn't. that wld have been inappropriate.

mad maddie:	how was the zombie crawl?
zoegirl:	awesome. but now I'm tired. y-a-w-n.
zoegirl:	how was the lecture?
mad maddie:	not as gory as I'd hoped, but I sat next to a girl named Jordan, and she seemed cool.
zoegirl:	was she thirteen?
mad maddie:	yes, and she still is.
mad maddie:	haha. that was funny! don't you think that was funny?
mad maddie:	whatever. no, not thirteen. a freshman like me. g'night!

Fri, Nov 1, 1:01 AM E.D.T.

SnowAngel:	u guys. omigod. I am SHAKING.
SnowAngel:	the Halloween mixer? not. good.
SnowAngel:	in fact, super scary, but not fun-scary. horrible-scary.
SnowAngel:	whoa. my hands literally won't stop shaking, which is making it hard to txt.
SnowAngel:	I just . . . I'll tell u more tomorrow.
SnowAngel:	but it's bad.

Fri, Nov 1, 8:05 AM E.D.T.

zoegirl:	Angela, are you ok???
zoegirl:	txting from class, which I have from now till noon. plz txt as soon as you can.
zoegirl:	I'm worried about you!

Fri, Nov 1, 10:30 AM E.D.T.

SnowAngel:	I'm ok, Zoe. I mean, I'm not dead or anything.
SnowAngel:	can you talk?
zoegirl:	no, but I can txt if I'm sneaky. what happened??
zoegirl:	were ppl at the party mean to Reid?
SnowAngel:	omg, I'd forgotten about that part. now it seems so irrelevant.

SnowAngel:	um, my fellow pledges were mainly nice to him. Anna was nice, and so was her boyfriend. but some of the older Zetas gave me/us a definite cold vibe.
SnowAngel:	one girl, Pierce, pulled me aside and asked if Reid had dressed up like a loser on purpose, and this other girl asked fake-sweetly if we were at the wrong party. so stupid.
zoegirl:	**these girls DO know they're in college, right? that they shld be above that stuff?**
SnowAngel:	apparently not. but in my mind, Reid was the HERO of the night, not that anyone but me knows
zoegirl:	**huh?**
SnowAngel:	night started off fine, other than the occasional cold look/snide remark. party was goofy, lots of dry ice and silly-spooky music and awesome decorations. LOTS of punch/beer/hard liquor too. ppl got crazy drunk.
zoegirl:	**did you?**
SnowAngel:	I had two beers, tops, and Reid isn't much of a drinker. he's not *against* drinking, but he has an uncle who's an alcoholic, so he wants to be careful.
SnowAngel:	so Reid, me, Anna, and her boyfriend were laughing and having fun. then Anna had to use the bathroom, which, as I've told u, is a monumental task in a frat house cuz of long lines. and plus she was in a box.
zoegirl:	**a box?**
SnowAngel:	she dressed up as a refrigerator. best. costume. ever.
SnowAngel:	so she and her bf went off together—buddy system! yay!—and then it was just me and Reid. well, and hundreds of drunk ppl dressed up as vampires and sumo wrestlers and strippers and stuff.
SnowAngel:	Reid said, "wanna walk around?" and I said, "sure," and he took my hand, and that part was tingly-happy-smiley.

zoegirl:	aw. so happy for you!
SnowAngel:	yeah, well, happy-smiley is about to go away.
zoegirl:	😦
SnowAngel:	uh-huh
SnowAngel:	the frat house was huge and crammed with ppl, but Reid and I wanted to find somewhere private, so we kept searching and peeking into different rooms and jumping away to avoid sloshing beer. that sort of thing.
SnowAngel:	and . . . well . . .
SnowAngel:	we did find a private spot. only we weren't the only ones who found it, and we weren't the first ones to have found it.
zoegirl:	meaning what?
SnowAngel:	it was way back past the laundry room. there were stacked-up cardboard boxes and some trophies and a rolled-up rug, so maybe a storage area?
zoegirl:	I have a bad feeling about this.
SnowAngel:	yeahhhhh
SnowAngel:	and before I even tell you the rest, I've made my decision about whether to officially join the Greek system or not, and the answer is NOT.
SnowAngel:	I'm depledging. after today, I'll no longer be a Zeta.
zoegirl:	Angela! what happened? who was already in the storage area?
SnowAngel:	I don't know names. three frat guys wearing face paint and dressed up like characters that were maybe from comic books, and one girl in a slutty nurse costume.
zoegirl:	uh-oh
SnowAngel:	she was facedown on the floor, totally passed out. I cld see that she was breathing, but she was unconscious.
SnowAngel:	and you've figured out the rest, haven't you?

zoegirl:	omg
zoegirl:	shit
SnowAngel:	it was soooooo bad, Zoe. her skirt was hiked up past her waist and one of the guys was tugging her underwear off. the lace got caught on the heel of her shoe, and I can't make that image go away. lacy underwear and a black high heel and a guy laughing in an awful drunk way.
zoegirl:	did they see you? the frat guys? what did y'all DO?
zoegirl:	I feel sick. I really really hope you called campus police.
SnowAngel:	kind of, but it was all happening RIGHT THEN.
SnowAngel:	I stepped all the way into the room and said, "quit it, you assholes! leave her alone!"
SnowAngel:	for a second they all froze, but they were super drunk, and I was wearing my stupid dead-princess outfit, and they said rude things, and it was awful. also my dress had some on-purpose rips in it already, and one of the guys just walked right over to me and jerked on the fabric to make it tear more. He was laughing like it was all a joke.
zoegirl:	Angela! you must have been so scared!
SnowAngel:	now I am, when I think about it, but right then I was just furious. I pushed the guy away and told Reid to call 911, and then I knelt by the girl and fixed her skirt. I *hated* seeing her with her skirt up like that.
SnowAngel:	she was just so vulnerable, and she didn't even know any of it was going on.
zoegirl:	jesus. thank god y'all happened to find her!
SnowAngel:	well, but a green frat boy—green cuz of his face paint—whacked Reid's phone out of his hand and said, "c'mon, let's get out of here" to his friends.
SnowAngel:	they all stormed past Reid, who was trying to block the way, but Reid did manage to get the girl's

	panties back. the guy who'd pulled them off was holding them like a fucking prize, and Reid held out his hand and said, "hey. be decent."
SnowAngel:	Reid said that, just for a second, the guy looked the tiniest bit ashamed. then he thrust the panties at Reid and shoved him hard on the shoulder before catching up with his asshole friends.
zoegirl:	good for Reid.
zoegirl:	and good for you too! sounds like *you* were the hero last night!
SnowAngel:	huh?
zoegirl:	earlier you said that Reid was the hero, but I think you both were. you did something really brave, Angela. not everyone would have.
SnowAngel:	I didn't choose to, tho, if that makes sense. I just DID.
zoegirl:	exactly
zoegirl:	but that poor girl!
zoegirl:	did someone put something in her drink or did she just pass out from plain drunkenness?
SnowAngel:	no idea
SnowAngel:	and if she was using the buddy system rule, her buddy did a crap job.
zoegirl:	thank god you and Reid came along before anything worse happened—not that what happened isn't already awful.
zoegirl:	are you going to turn those guys in?
SnowAngel:	how wld I? "three guys in comic book costumes assaulted a girl, and one of them was green?"
zoegirl:	you have to do *something*
SnowAngel:	I know. I just don't know what. I'm going to talk to Anna later today and see if she has any advice.
zoegirl:	you should talk to the girl you saved. maybe she knows who the guys were.
SnowAngel:	yeah, only I don't know who she is either.

zoegirl:	???
zoegirl:	isn't she in your sorority?
SnowAngel:	yeah, but I don't know every single Zeta. I don't even know every single pledge.
zoegirl:	you didn't recognize her at all?
SnowAngel:	um, no. as I said. are you trying to make me feel bad?
zoegirl:	no no no no no! you saved her, that's the only thing that matters. God, Angela. hugs and hugs and hugs!!!

Fri, Nov 1, 1:36 PM P.D.T.

mad maddie:	**hey, Angela, answer yr phone.**
mad maddie:	**ANSWER! I read your texts.**
mad maddie:	**ok, I'm calling again . . .**
mad maddie:	**dammit, Angela, ANSWER YR FUCKING PHONE!**
SnowAngel:	shhhhh! I'm here, k?
SnowAngel:	I'm at the Zeta house. I told my pledge class leader that I was depledging, and she said I have to talk to the president of the chapter.
SnowAngel:	so now I'm sitting outside a room, waiting, while the two of them talk.
mad maddie:	**are you ok? are you going to tell her about the girl you saved?**
mad maddie:	**also, how'd you get her home? you never said.**
SnowAngel:	Reid and I slung her arms over our shoulders and walked/carried her to the Zeta house.
SnowAngel:	she was groggy, but she kind of stumbled along between us. at one point she asked about her stethoscope.
mad maddie:	**her stethoscope?**
SnowAngel:	nurse? Halloween?
mad maddie:	**oh yeah**
SnowAngel:	once we got to the Zeta house, I didn't know what

to do. didn't know her name, didn't know if she lived in the Zeta house, didn't even know for sure if she was a Zeta.

mad maddie: **how cld you not know if she's a Zeta?**

SnowAngel: god, you and Zoe seriously don't get it.

SnowAngel: there are 250 active sisters on campus. I was supposed to memorize their names and faces for pledge stuff, but I didn't, ok?

mad maddie: **ok! sorry!**

SnowAngel: do you know everyone in yr dorm? cld you recognize them in a lineup?

mad maddie: **I said I'm sorry. I understand now, so go on.**

SnowAngel: well, I tried to think what I'd want someone to do for me if the situation was reversed.

mad maddie: **the situation never will be reversed. don't ever let that happen to you, Angela.**

SnowAngel: I wldn't want everyone knowing about it unless I chose to tell them. more importantly, I'd want to know that I *hadn't* been raped.

mad maddie: **agh. but yes. me too.**

SnowAngel: we ended up tucking her into a bed in an empty bedroom. we wrote a note and left it for her, along with her underwear. we tucked both into a pocket on her nurse outfit, with the note sticking out just a little so she'd see it.

mad maddie: **what did the note say?**

SnowAngel: "you're ok. no one hurt you."

SnowAngel: I wanted to add "but next time, please don't get so drunk," but I didn't want her to feel like what happened was her fault or that she was being blamed.

mad maddie: **plus, someone cld have slipped a roofie into her drink. it DOES happen.**

SnowAngel:	I also wanted to tell her how sorry I was, but I cldn't find the right words. so I kept it short and sweet.
mad maddie:	**I think you did right by her. I think you handled it in the best way you could.**
mad maddie:	**so *are* you going to tell the Zeta prez?**
SnowAngel:	I don't know! but I don't think so, cuz like I said, I'd want it to stay private if it was me.
SnowAngel:	yikes, they're calling me in, wish me luck!
mad maddie:	**good luck, good luck! not that u need it. I'm so proud, my friend!** 💜 💜 💜

Sat, Nov 2, 4:03 PM E.D.T.

zoegirl:	sending hugs to both of you.
zoegirl:	wanted you to know I'm thinking about you!

Sun, Nov 3, 7:00 PM E.S.T.

SnowAngel:	the Cross Over ceremony is probably starting at the Zeta house. this is when I'd be becoming a full-fledged member . . . if I hadn't depledged.
zoegirl:	how are you doing? are you still ok with your decision?
SnowAngel:	mainly. my feelings are a bit mixed up.
zoegirl:	I can understand that. you had fun with those girls. you made some true friends.
SnowAngel:	Anna's the only girl I'm going to miss, really.
zoegirl:	you can still do stuff with her, can't you?
SnowAngel:	yeah, I guess.
SnowAngel:	but it won't be the same. sororities take up a lot of yr life. there isn't always room for other stuff or even other ppl.
zoegirl:	😞
zoegirl:	I'm sorry, Angela.
SnowAngel:	thx 😞 😞 😞

zoegirl:	have you heard anything new about the girl from the party?
SnowAngel:	no, and I haven't seen her on campus or anything. I described her to Anna to see if Anna knew her, but "skinny and blond" describes almost all the Zetas.
SnowAngel:	Anna said she'd keep her ears open, tho. she told me she has a cousin who was date-raped, and that her cousin still hasn't gotten over it.
zoegirl:	I'm not sure that's something anyone ever gets over.
zoegirl:	agh, I just got the chills again, imagining what might have happened if you and Reid hadn't shown up when you did.
SnowAngel:	but we did
zoegirl:	but you did.

Mon, Nov 4, 2:00 PM E.S.T.

SnowAngel:	helloooo, Maddie. I think I'm supposed to be in this mysterious "geology lab" I keep hearing vague references to, but it's far too confusing. why wld being enrolled in one class require you to have to go to a second class?
SnowAngel:	it's like going to the dentist and getting yr teeth cleaned and then being told to go to some weird other place to get yr new toothbrush.
mad maddie:	**u realize yr going to fail geology . . .**
SnowAngel:	no way, silly. my geology professor loves me.
SnowAngel:	all of my professors love me, because I am an excellent class participator.
mad maddie:	**when yr not txting, that iOS**
mad maddie:	***is**
SnowAngel:	when I'm not texting that iOS. exactly.
mad maddie:	😊

SnowAngel:	ANYway, I fear my soul is being sucked away. must stop being addicted to Twitter!
mad maddie:	**and tumblr and FB and Instagram . . . shld I go on?**
SnowAngel:	I checked on our friend Jana, and she's not a happy camper. wanna hear more?
mad maddie:	**no**
mad maddie:	**but ok, sure.**
SnowAngel:	all of her recent tweets have been about how depressed she is, how stupid college is, and how she wants to drop out.
mad maddie:	**maybe she shld.**
SnowAngel:	what? why wld you say that?
mad maddie:	**cuz going to college just cuz yr expected to doesn't make a ton of sense, not when u think about it.**
SnowAngel:	but . . . college! learning stuff and getting smarter! it's important!
mad maddie:	**which is why yr skipping yr geology lab again. nice.**
SnowAngel:	ok, but there's other stuff too. college isn't JUST about book learning.
mad maddie:	**my point exactly. you can teach yrself anything you really need to know by going to the library.**
SnowAngel:	why are you arguing on Jana's side? I *like* college. don't you?
mad maddie:	**dude. what idiot doesn't like college?**
SnowAngel:	aargh! you are being very aggravating!!!

Tues, Nov 5, 3:47 PM E.S.T.

SnowAngel:	what's crack-a-lackin, homeslice?
zoegirl:	trying to finish short story about a girl who is like Icarus and sprouts wings, only I don't want her to end up flying too close to the sun.
SnowAngel:	no. wldn't want that.
zoegirl:	really need to work. sorry!

mad maddie: **oooo-eeee! makin' bacon!**

SnowAngel: yr so weird

SnowAngel: oh, look, Carrie Benway's dog snuck up behind her and sniffed her neck.

mad maddie: ***I'm* weird?**

SnowAngel: I don't even know who Carrie Benway is.

SnowAngel: do we know who Carrie Benway is?

mad maddie: **she's the girl with the sneaky dog, ya dum-dum.**
😊

SnowAngel: and . . . *double-tasks to read Twitter feed* . . . Justine Schu is helping to get the chores of the world done. huh. that is perplexing to me on many levels.

mad maddie: **who's Justine Schu?**

SnowAngel: I have no clue. how did all these ppl I don't know end up on my Twitter feed????

mad maddie: ***cuffs Angela fondly on cheek***

mad maddie: **cuz yr so darn likable. it's cute.**

SnowAngel: you're in a good mood today. what's up?

mad maddie: **Thanksgiving break is getting closer. what can I say?**

SnowAngel: and sweetpea252 is going to have sex on a Popsicle. lovely.

mad maddie: **what about Jana? any news on Jana?**

SnowAngel: well, let's see . . .

SnowAngel: Jana Whitaker is going to cut and dye her hair— or maybe she already has.

SnowAngel: she posted some selfies, and . . . aye-yai-yai. I wonder if she seriously is trying to self-destruct, cuz her haircut is more of a chop, and the color is bright orange. bright BRIGHT orange. what was she thinking?

mad maddie: **she needs your Fashion Rescue services.**

SnowAngel:	she certainly does. oh, which reminds me! guess what?
mad maddie:	**what?**
SnowAngel:	the girl Reid and I rescued must have told someone what happened, which is good, cuz . . . well, cuz you can't keep the bad stuff in. you have to share or you'll implode.
mad maddie:	**how do you know she told?**
SnowAngel:	Anna says there was a chapter meeting about it. no names, and it doesn't sound like anyone's going to be turned in, but the Zetas are axing that particular fraternity from all social engagements for the rest of the year.
mad maddie:	**the whole rest of the year. wow, that must sting.**
SnowAngel:	yeah, I know. but.
SnowAngel:	at least it's out there. and Anna said everyone took it seriously, and that the Zeta president used the whole meeting to talk about party safety and all that.
mad maddie:	**and those guys get off scot-free. yay!**
SnowAngel:	that part sucks. but maybe they woke up the next morning and felt hugely guilty. I sure hope so.
mad maddie:	**I hope so too. I'm just not nearly as optimistic.**
mad maddie:	**but Angela? you did a GOOD THING. I love ya, lady.**
SnowAngel:	*melts*
SnowAngel:	I love you too, Mads. forever and ever and ever. 💜

Thu, Nov 7, 5:33 PM E.S.T.

SnowAngel:	dudes!!!! I am so happy! I went to Shakes Alive with Reid today—we held hands, yummy-yummy, and we kissed, yummy-yummier—and guess what?
SnowAngel:	WE SAW JERMAINE!!!!
SnowAngel:	do you two remember Jermaine? the guy who lived in my dorm room for a while?

mad maddie:	**I remember that quite clearly, yes.**
zoegirl:	I, too, will never forget.
SnowAngel:	well, he's working at Shakes Alive. he got a job! at Shakes Alive!
zoegirl:	Angela, that's awesome.
mad maddie:	**does that mean he'll give u free milkshakes?**
SnowAngel:	ooo, maybe
SnowAngel:	he gave me a HUGE smile when he saw me, and he cldn't talk for long, but he's doing so much better. and the Lutheran church is doing a community-wide Thanksgiving meal, so he's going to that, which means he won't be alone on Thanksgiving!
SnowAngel:	all sorts of things to be thankful for, yeah? ⭐
zoegirl:	absolutely. like being brave because a certain friend made us swear to be!
SnowAngel:	how were you brave, or is the braveness yet to happen?
zoegirl:	it's yet to happen. I'm going to an open mic night tonight at a coffeehouse called the Cup & Chaucer. if I get up enough courage, I might read one of my short stories.
SnowAngel:	the burning girl one?
zoegirl:	if Holly reads one of hers, then I promised I'd read one of mine too. eek—but exciting.
SnowAngel:	yr turn, M-boogie. what r u thankful for?
mad maddie:	**um . . .**
mad maddie:	**toilet paper. I'm thankful for toilet paper.**
SnowAngel:	Maddie!
mad maddie:	**what? I am! also salt. also fingernails, and before u scold me, think about it. FINGERNAILS ARE AWESOME.**
SnowAngel:	ok, Maddie. ok. *pats Maddie on the head*
mad maddie:	**and I'm thankful for Thanksgiving break, ya dum-dum head!** 😊

mad maddie: soooooooooooooooooooooo—*takes breath*—ooooooo excited.

zoegirl: me too

SnowAngel: me three

zoegirl: it's time for me to meet Holly, so I've got to go.

mad maddie: yeah, I'm outta here too. tootles.

SnowAngel: smoochie-smoochie! 😘 😘 😘

Thu, Nov 7, 10:20 PM E.S.T.

zoegirl: I read my short story at the open mic night, just so y'all know. out loud, in front of thousands of my closest friends.

zoegirl: twenty of my closest friends?

zoegirl: ok, two of my closest friends (at least here at Kenyon) (Holly and Gannon) and eighteen random people.

zoegirl: but I did it, and everyone applauded, and I'm so giddy, I feel like spinning around in circles! 💫

Thu, Nov 7, 8:45 PM P.S.T.

mad maddie: whoa. all that and still in bed before—*does quick time change calculation on fingers*—before eleven!

mad maddie: u go, girl!

Sat, Nov 9, 5:00 PM E.S.T.

zoegirl: omigod. this is TOO BIZARRE

zoegirl: GUESS WHO JUST CALLED ME????? out of the blue! saying he MISSED me and had made a huge mistake and was just confused about life and lonely and didn't know what he was doing?????

SnowAngel: no!

SnowAngel: no.

SnowAngel:	NO.
mad maddie:	**did he mention Canyon?**
zoegirl:	I saw his name pop up on my phone and my heart STOPPED.
zoegirl:	I almost didn't answer. my body did that hot-cold-hot-cold thing and my knees went wobbly. I mean, it was just DOUG, but the Doug I knew seems so far away from the Doug who exists now.
SnowAngel:	what did he say? was it good or bad?
zoegirl:	it was confusing. not good or bad, but definitely confusing.
mad maddie:	**explain**
zoegirl:	sigh
zoegirl:	it was painful to hear his voice. painful to realize for sure (and the way I realized for sure is because my body told me) that I didn't want to get back together with him, although that's ALL I wanted when he first broke up with me.
mad maddie:	**so what changed b/w then and now?**
zoegirl:	oh, you know. everything. Holly and Gannon and going running every morning. being brave and reading aloud at the coffeehouse.
zoegirl:	I'm happy, or at least happyish.
zoegirl:	no—I really am happy, and *this* is my life now. the thought of slipping back into loving someone but never seeing him, not truly knowing what HIS life is like, not truly being part of his life . . .
SnowAngel:	you wld have felt like you were regressing
zoegirl:	exactly. but this is DOUG we're talking about.
zoegirl:	the whole thing played with my mind.
mad maddie:	**what about Doug? is he doing ok?**
zoegirl:	yeah, I guess. he didn't fall apart and start sobbing or anything.

zoegirl:	he wants to get together over Thanksgiving break, just to hang out.
SnowAngel:	and?
zoegirl:	and I said sure—but as friends. but I didn't say the "friends" part out loud because it would have sounded so cliche.
zoegirl:	so if a hanging-out situation comes up, y'all are coming with me, k?
SnowAngel:	of course!
SnowAngel:	*hugs Zoe from across the space-time continuum*
SnowAngel:	I think you handled it really well, babes.
mad maddie:	**true dat. our little Zoe's growing up.**

Sun, Nov 10, 5:01 PM E.S.T.

SnowAngel:	o.
SnowAngel:	m.
SnowAngel:	g.
SnowAngel:	Zoe's life has become nutso. yesterday Doug called her, right? well, guess who called her *today*?
SnowAngel:	Canyon! the girl who lives on his hall! 😮
SnowAngel:	she SAID she was calling cuz Doug's her friend and she cares about him and hates to see him sad. she SAID she really hoped Zoe wld give him another chance.
SnowAngel:	but doesn't that sound almost fake-nice? fake-concerned?
SnowAngel:	if she's that worried, she shld just comfort Doug herself.
SnowAngel:	or maybe she did, at one point, AND THEN SHE BROKE UP WITH HIM! and that's why he called Zoe!
SnowAngel:	but Zo didn't answer. Canyon left a message, and Zo isn't planning on calling her back.
SnowAngel:	COLLEGE IS SO WEIRD!!!!

mad maddie: just checking in with my girls to pass on a very important public service announcement:

mad maddie: happy Monday! 😛

mad maddie: tick tick, tock tock, Thanksgiving break's just around the clock . . .

mad maddie: I can't wait!

mad maddie: hi, ladies! *waves*

mad maddie: happy Tuesday! 😛

mad maddie: where are y'all, ya big lugs? yr not, like, studying or sumpin, are ya?

mad maddie: well, whatevs. call me. text me. send me some of that good ol' winsome threesome loving!

mad maddie: until then . . . happy Tuesday! 😛

zoegirl: NOT happy Tuesday. not for me. very very sad Tuesday. 😔

zoegirl: maybe I'm overreacting. I don't know. but I need to talk, and neither of you are answering your phones.

zoegirl: call me!!!!

SnowAngel: Zo! just saw this. txting instead of calling cuz I'm at Starbucks, and I have very strong opinions about how ppl shldn't hold phone convos in public places.

SnowAngel: what's wrong???

zoegirl: you know my creative writing class that I love so much? my professor said I suck, and that I'll never be a writer, and that I should give up now and never take another writing class again.

zoegirl:	I'm not kidding. she did!
SnowAngel:	she did not. what really happened?
zoegirl:	in class she passed out access codes for registering for CW 200, which is the next creative writing class. only the creative writing track is a "selective" track, meaning your professor has to say you're good enough if you want to keep going.
zoegirl:	like, the first creative writing class you can just sign up for. but after that, you have to get permission.
SnowAngel:	but Zoe, yr an amazing writer. there's no way yr prof didn't pick u to go on.
zoegirl:	except she didn't!
zoegirl:	she announced at the beginning of class that she knew we all wanted to go on to the next level, but that unfortunately that's not the way it works and it wasn't within her power to change the system.
zoegirl:	then she passed out the access codes—right then and there—and *everyone* in the class got one except for me and a girl named Stephanie.
zoegirl:	and do you know what Stephanie writes about? bugs! every single short story she wrote was told from the point of view of an aphid! I AM NOT KIDDING!
zoegirl:	so Bug Girl and I, we're the ones who suck. we're the only two kids in the whole class who are such bad writers that we're not allowed to keep writing!!!!
SnowAngel:	Zoe! oh, honey!!!!!!!
SnowAngel:	(((((((((((((HUGS!)))))))))))))
SnowAngel:	cld u go talk to her or something? yr prof?
zoegirl:	yeah, right. NO WAY.
SnowAngel:	but you ARE a good writer. it's got to be some kind of mistake.

zoegirl:	it wasn't. my professor gave me this sad, pitying look and squeezed my shoulder, as if to say, "so sorry, I know this is a tough blow."
zoegirl:	maybe she was trying to be nice, I don't know. but all it did was make me that much closer to crying.
SnowAngel:	ack. Zo. I am SO sorry.
SnowAngel:	ah, crap—Maddie calling. one sec . . .
zoegirl:	Angela?
zoegirl:	come back! I thought you said no phone calls in public places, so get off the phone with Maddie and come back to me!
SnowAngel:	Zoe. SHIT.
SnowAngel:	starting new txt thread so Mads can be part of it, but prepare yrself: it's bad!!!!

Tues, Nov 12, 7:23 PM E.S.T.

SnowAngel:	all right, Mads. shld I tell her or do you want to?
zoegirl:	what's going on???
mad maddie:	**my parents. they hate me**
zoegirl:	what?
SnowAngel:	they don't hate her.
SnowAngel:	they don't HATE you, Maddie. in fact I'm sure they feel absolutely terrible.
SnowAngel:	but Zoe, they're not letting Maddie come home for Thanksgiving!!!
zoegirl:	WHAT?
mad maddie:	**yeah, I know, that's great, huh? might as well kill myself now.**
SnowAngel:	MADDIE. don't you even say that.
SnowAngel:	and Zoe, they've all of a sudden decided they don't have enough $ for her plane ticket.
zoegirl:	didn't they already buy it? Thanksgiving break is in a week and a half!
mad maddie:	**yes, but then they took this stupid financial**

	planning class. they've decided to live a "cash-based life," and since the ticket was exchangeable, they exchanged it.
mad maddie:	now—if I live that long—it'll be my stupid coming-home-for-Christmas ticket.
mad maddie:	GOD. they hate me—and I hate them!
SnowAngel:	what did Ian say?
mad maddie:	
SnowAngel:	Maddie?
mad maddie:	
zoegirl:	Maddie, you're sending text bubbles with no texts in them. that is not helpful.
mad maddie:	fuck helpful. fuck everything. I can't even talk about it right now, so good-fucking-bye.

Wed, Nov 13, 7:24 AM E.S.T.

zoegirl:	I just ran five miles nonstop. I have never done that before.
zoegirl:	I think I ran for so long because I had so many things to process.
zoegirl:	1) Doug,
zoegirl:	2) being axed from the creative writing program, and
zoegirl:	3) Maddie.
zoegirl:	of all of them, Maddie's the biggest. so I was thinking . . . could WE buy her a ticket?
zoegirl:	she really needs to come home. she kept saying how that was the only thing keeping her going, you know?
zoegirl:	so, I don't know. throwing it out there.
zoegirl:	all right, I've got to shower. talk soon!

Thu, Nov 14, 2:45 PM E.S.T.

SnowAngel:	so now all Maddie will say, when she bothers to

	answer her phone, is what a total loser and failure she is.
SnowAngel:	it's driving me bonkers!
zoegirl:	me too, BECAUSE I WANT TO FIX EVERYTHING FOR HER AND I CAN'T!
zoegirl:	I've got exactly $123.07 in my bank account, and that's it.
SnowAngel:	and I'm so rich, I have 32 whole dollars and some random cents.
SnowAngel:	so that, combined with what I've got, brings us to . . .
zoegirl:	$155, give or take
SnowAngel:	it is annoying how fast you do math
zoegirl:	it is annoying how poor you are!
zoegirl:	kidding. kind of.
zoegirl:	I've searched the airline sites, as well as ones like Travelocity and Kayak, and the cheapest ticket I can find costs $461.
zoegirl:	oh, and that's just for one-way. a round-trip ticket is $589.
SnowAngel:	but we can't give up. Maddie's seriously depressed, Zoe.
zoegirl:	I know. I asked if maybe she could spend Thanksgiving with one of her suitemates, and she said she'd rather stay in the homeless shelter.
SnowAngel:	with Jermaine!
SnowAngel:	nvm, bad joke.
SnowAngel:	it's a strange thing for her to say, tho, cuz Maddie used to like her suitemates . . . didn't she? and now she dislikes them so much that she'd rather eat turkey with sad dirty ppl?
zoegirl:	well, things with Zara and the Esbees have been going downhill. even so, I'm sure she was just being dramatic.
zoegirl:	have you talked to Ian?

SnowAngel:	briefly, but he had class. do that math magic of yrs and tell me how much we need to buy her that ticket, on top of what we already have.
zoegirl:	$4.34, and my stupid parents say that they "can't interfere with the decisions Maddie's parents have made," so there goes that possibility.
SnowAngel:	mine said the same thing. my mom said she'd be happy to help if Maddie's parents asked her to, but that she doesn't want to go to them offering money because of dumb "I'm sure they don't want charity" reasons.
zoegirl:	when we are parents, we will help our kids when they need help! promise?
SnowAngel:	duh!
SnowAngel:	Ian will be more than happy to chip in, I'm sure, but I doubt he'll have that much. how can we raise $400???
zoegirl:	I don't know. is it even possible for us to raise $400?
SnowAngel:	Shut. Your. Mouth.
SnowAngel:	oh dear. did that sound harsh? I don't mean to sound harsh—I just don't want to think anything but positive thoughts!
zoegirl:	I want to get Maddie to Atlanta as much as you do, but we can't just snap our fingers and make it happen.
SnowAngel:	so then, what? are you suggesting we give up?
SnowAngel:	WE ARE THE WINSOME THREESOME! WE DO *NOT* GIVE UP!
zoegirl:	but Angela . . .
SnowAngel:	what happened to the Zoe I used to know? where's the spirit? where's the guts?!!!
zoegirl:	whose guts?
SnowAngel:	*your* guts, stupid!

zoegirl:	um, am I normally a girl with spirit and guts?
SnowAngel:	yes. no. kind of!
zoegirl:	I'm the quiet girl in the corner, Angela. I'm quiet and I read books. remember?
SnowAngel:	but you still have spirit and guts, like how you got over Doug by becoming a runner and how you kiss girls and how you got up in front of millions of ppl and read yr story. all of that. takes. guts!
zoegirl:	I'm hardly a runner, I kissed ONE girl, and I got kicked out of my writing class. I got told I *couldn't* be a writer, remember?
SnowAngel:	Zoe, you're being annoying. your teacher can tell you that you can't take the next creative writing class, but she can't tell you not to write.
zoegirl:	oh
SnowAngel:	yes, and what does she know anyway?
SnowAngel:	if you want to be a writer, then you'll keep writing, because that's WHAT YOU DO. you don't give up.
zoegirl:	what are you leading up to?
SnowAngel:	that we're not giving up on Maddie either. that we'll get her to Atlanta one way or another!

Thu, Nov 14, 8:12 PM E.S.T.

SnowAngel:	Maddie, pick up the phone.
SnowAngel:	Maddie!
SnowAngel:	Pick! Up! The! Phone!
SnowAngel:	*rips hair out*
SnowAngel:	will u at least txt me back, then????
SnowAngel:	cuz girl, I talked to Ian, and you have some explaining to do. BIG TIME.
SnowAngel:	plus I am worried about you and I love you and I am worried about you! 😶
SnowAngel:	goddammit, Maddie. call or txt when u can.
SnowAngel:	I'll be waiting. 🙁

SnowAngel: Zo! I found Ian yesterday, and guess what?

zoegirl: what? does he have piles of money hidden away that we can use to buy a plane ticket?

SnowAngel: no, and he thought it was weird that I even asked.

SnowAngel: not weird as if it was a bad idea. weird cuz he had no idea how upset Maddie is.

zoegirl: how cld he not know how upset . . . ?

zoegirl: duh duh duh. because she's been keeping it from him. truly keeping it from him, even more than I could have imagined.

zoegirl: Angela, I'm starting to wonder if Ian knew *any* of it. did he know that Maddie and Zara don't hang out anymore?

SnowAngel: I mentioned that to him, just in terms of ". . . yeah, and she's not going out with her friends, and she's not even sure they ARE friends . . ."

SnowAngel: he gave me the blankest look and said he didn't think she'd ever really gone out with them.

zoegirl: what???

SnowAngel: so I told him about the casino and the roller derby and the other insane adventures she's had, and he knew about NONE of them.

SnowAngel: he thought I was making stuff up to mess with him. he thought I was just being random!

SnowAngel: is Maddie hiding stuff from us too? is she leading a double life???

zoegirl: I don't know, but if I had to guess, I'd guess yes.

SnowAngel: P.S. Ian can contribute $150 to Project Save Maddie, which is awesome. but that still leaves us short, doesn't it?

SnowAngel: and confused!!!

SnowAngel: P.P.S. and also, that girl from the party? the nurse, on Halloween?

SnowAngel: this has nothing to do with Maddie, but she's going to be ok(ish), and I wanted to tell you.

SnowAngel: Anna heard some girls talking at the Zeta house, and she found out that the girl who dressed up as a nurse is a junior named Kylie.

SnowAngel: Anna talked to her, and Kylie wasn't exactly thrilled, but she didn't turn Anna away either. she said she'd rather not know.

SnowAngel: anyway, Kylie is seeing a counselor. she's not dropping out of school or anything and she's staying in the sorority, even. Anna said that Kylie looked bewildered when Anna asked that question, like she didn't see how the two things connected.

SnowAngel: maybe they don't for her. but for me they did.

SnowAngel: but this next part makes me happy. Kylie told Anna it meant a lot, the note. knowing that she hadn't been . . .

SnowAngel: 🌑

SnowAngel: knowing that it cld have been worse, but wasn't.

SnowAngel: *deep breath*

SnowAngel: ok. done. thought you'd want to know, that's all.

zoegirl: Maddie, plz be awake.

SnowAngel: yeah, Maddie. we know you don't want to talk. whatever. but YOU know you're being stupid (I love you!) and self-sabotaging (still love you! will always love you!)

zoegirl: me too, Mads. love and love, even though you have some major explaining to do. but right now that doesn't matter. we just want to know you're ok.

SnowAngel:	type a dot or something if yr there.
zoegirl:	a dot? do you mean a period?
SnowAngel:	a dot or a period or anything! the tic-tac-toe board, even.
SnowAngel:	###
SnowAngel:	see how easy?
zoegirl:	that's not a tic-tac-toe board, Angela. you do know that, right?
zoegirl:	but never mind. Maddie's not typing anything, so . . .
SnowAngel:	I think we shld tell her anyway.
SnowAngel:	I hope you're reading this right now, Maddie!!! BECAUSE IT IS IMPORTANT!
SnowAngel:	Zoe? you start.
zoegirl:	well, Angela and I Skyped for hours last night. at the end, we added Ian to the call too.
zoegirl:	and we put it all together—all the stories you told us.
SnowAngel:	we know they're not true, not a single one.
SnowAngel:	which means u were lying to us 😞
zoegirl:	a lot
SnowAngel:	and when we figured it out, we felt pretty dumb. because remember that one time when I even said to you, "Whoa, Maddie, your life is like a movie"? haha, you must have laughed yr head off at that.
zoegirl:	or not. I tossed and turned all night, and it came to me finally that you probably *wanted* us to figure it out, and maybe you've been sad that it's taken us this long.
SnowAngel:	we made a list:
SnowAngel:	first u told Zoe that you were a card player with mad skills. we had to IMDb that one after we figured out the others, cuz I've never seen it. Zoe has, but it was a long time ago.

SnowAngel:	anyway, you got that from the movie about the genius MIT kids who figured out how to rip off casinos by counting cards, didn't u?
zoegirl:	"21"
zoegirl:	that's what the movie was called
SnowAngel:	then came your stint as a roller derby queen. I still can't believe Zoe believed that.
zoegirl:	well, you believed me when I told you about it, Angela.
zoegirl:	and can't you see Maddie as a roller derby queen?
zoegirl:	you'd be a fabulous roller derby queen, Mads. you'd rock those high sports socks, and you look awesome in pigtails.
SnowAngel:	that was from "Whip It," right? about the girl who felt like a freak in her small town but made new freak friends in a roller derby league?
zoegirl:	and then you almost went surfing, but there was a shark alert. "Soul Surfer"? about the girl who got her arm bitten off?
SnowAngel:	I 🖤 that movie, btw.
zoegirl:	and then right around the time Doug broke up with me, you magically became a character in "The Hangover," from the scene when the guys woke up in a hotel room and found a tiger in the bathroom.
SnowAngel:	a tiger that they had to return to that scary dude, which is what you claimed that you and Zara and the Esbees were doing.
SnowAngel:	jesus, Zoe. we really *were* stupid, weren't we?
zoegirl:	yep. except . . . she's Maddie. she made it all sound possible.
zoegirl:	you ARE a good liar, Mads, though I'm not sure that's a skill to be proud of.
zoegirl:	and then the ghost hunting night. "Ghostbusters"?

"listen, I smell something"??? Ian told us that you two can shoot quotes back and forth from that movie forever.

SnowAngel: and then back to Vegas, sans tiger, only you didn't really get on the plane because—surprise!—the guy you were with was scared of flying and needed anxiety meds.

zoegirl: the three of us saw "Bridesmaids" together. God.

SnowAngel: and you laughed so hard when everyone got food poisoning from that sketchy Brazilian restaurant.

SnowAngel: I'm surprised u didn't claim u had to take a dump in the middle of the road.

zoegirl: and then, last but not least, Halloween. I did the zombie crawl, Angela went to a party, and you? you—supposedly—went to a lecture given by the son of a mad scientist WHO THOUGHT HE COULD REANIMATE DEAD PEOPLE.

zoegirl: omigosh.

zoegirl: Ian figured that one out, too. he said the two of you watched "Young Frankenstein" over the summer and loved it.

SnowAngel: which is awesome. yay, movies.

SnowAngel: but Maddie, your life *isn't* like a movie, is it? your life is stolen from a bunch of different movies.

zoegirl: it's you sitting around watching Netflix all the time.

zoegirl: AND it's you totally reneging on the yolo oath.

SnowAngel: but we're not here to yell at u. right, Zo?

zoegirl: no. but we are upset.

SnowAngel: VERY upset.

zoegirl: mainly we just want u to be ok.

SnowAngel: so be ok. please? 🙏

SnowAngel: and we ARE going to get u to Atlanta over

	Thanksgiving. we haven't worked out every last detail yet, but we will. tell her, Zoe.
zoegirl:	we will. Angela's stubborn, if you haven't noticed. she's forcing me to be gutsy and not give up (normally YOUR job!), so that's what I'm going to do. 👍
SnowAngel:	Zoe, Maddie's still not saying anything.
zoegirl:	no, she's not.
SnowAngel:	Maddie?
SnowAngel:	just one little dot? plz plz pretty plz?
SnowAngel:	. . .
SnowAngel:	. . .
zoegirl:	. . . .
SnowAngel:	le sigh. ☹
zoegirl:	we're here for you, Maddie. just know that.
SnowAngel:	🖤 🖤 🖤 🖤 🖤 🖤 🖤 🖤 🖤 🖤 🖤 🖤

Sun, Nov 17, 2:00 AM P.S.T.

mad maddie: .

Sun, Nov 17, 11:26 AM E.S.T.

zoegirl:	oh, Maddie, thank you for your middle-of-the-night text!!!
zoegirl:	I'll take your dots anytime. are you doing any better?
mad maddie:	not really. I keep listening to Mumford and Sons and feeling depressed.
zoegirl:	I love Mumford and Sons.
mad maddie:	that line about dying alone? yep, that's me.
mad maddie:	I know I'm being melodramatic, but I can't help it. everything sucks.
zoegirl:	oh, Maddie. 😞
zoegirl:	but the song isn't about dying alone. the song's about refusing to die alone.

mad maddie:	**it is?**
mad maddie:	**no it's not.**
zoegirl:	go check. look up the lyrics.
mad maddie:	**oh**
mad maddie:	**huh**
zoegirl:	and then later there's the part about no more tears and no more fears, and how everything will be ok.
mad maddie:	**whoa. it's an amazing song—it's gorgeous—but how weird that I heard it so differently than you.**
zoegirl:	well . . . you're depressed, like you said. even though you denied it two seconds later.
zoegirl:	but Angela and Ian and I *are* going to figure out a way to get you to Atlanta.
mad maddie:	**don't say that. it's not going to happen, and it just makes me feel bad, like I'm this deadweight you have to carry.**
zoegirl:	oh, hush
zoegirl:	anyway, you don't get a vote. we don't have quite enough money yet, but we're going to raise it somehow. I give you my word.
mad maddie:	**hmmm. dubious. but sweet gesture, Zo.**
zoegirl:	don't give up on us, and don't give up on you. promise?
mad maddie:	**can't promise. but I'll try.**
zoegirl:	that's my girl.
zoegirl:	🌷 🌷 🌷 🌷 🌷

Sun, Nov 17, 12:41 PM E.S.T.

zoegirl:	I texted Maddie this morning, and she RESPONDED! miracle of miracles! I gave her my word that we'd raise the money for her ticket, so now we have to.
SnowAngel:	we always had to.

zoegirl:	how are we going to raise the remaining $280???
SnowAngel:	by . . . doing something!
zoegirl:	yes, that's helpful. what sort of something?
SnowAngel:	a fundraiser? a Georgia/Ohio fundraiser for an excellent cause?
SnowAngel:	I can sell cupcakes on the quad. I'm sure Anna will help me, and I bet Lucy will too. altho I bet her cupcakes will be gross and filled with hemp seeds.
SnowAngel:	cld u do something like that too?
zoegirl:	I guess
zoegirl:	but $280 worth of cupcakes? in four days??? Maddie's last day of classes before break is this Friday, just like ours.
SnowAngel:	well, then snap to it!
SnowAngel:	call in all the troops u can think of: Holly, Gannon, whoever.
SnowAngel:	GO!

Tues, Nov 19, 3:50 PM E.S.T.

SnowAngel:	hi, Maddie! 🍭
SnowAngel:	just txting to give u a status report. all ships ahoy, matey! 🚢
SnowAngel:	altho—shh—I don't actually know what that means. ahoy? what's ahoy?
SnowAngel:	but in this case, just know that we're going to make sure Project Save Maddie is a total winner!

Tues, Nov 19, 3:54 PM E.S.T.

SnowAngel:	Zoe, Project Save Maddie is a total failure. I sold TWO DOZEN FRICKIN CUPCAKES this morning, and guess how much that made?
SnowAngel:	a whopping $9.25. yes, u heard me. nine dollars and twenty-five measly cents!
zoegirl:	but . . . that's less than a dollar per cupcake!

SnowAngel:	I made a sign that said "Cupcakes for the Cause! Pay What You Can, All Contributions Welcome!"
SnowAngel:	which, in retrospect, was possibly not the best strategy with a bunch of poor college students.
zoegirl:	well, Gannon, Holly, and I sat at a table in the student center and sold poems for five bucks apiece. only we didn't sell a single one, so you did better than we did.
SnowAngel:	not a high demand for on-the-spot poems?
zoegirl:	unfathomable. I know.
zoegirl:	but guess who I saw? MY CREATIVE WRITING PROFESSOR.
SnowAngel:	the horrible professor?
SnowAngel:	the one who said, "hey, you! you don't get to be a creative writing major!" that one?
zoegirl:	yep. she saw Holly and Gannon and me, and I know she did because I SAW her see us. and then she spun around and headed the opposite way.
SnowAngel:	wow. great role model for being an adult.
zoegirl:	yep. and then a crazy urge came over me, cuz I was with Holly, who is fearless, and cuz I was thinking about Mads, who is fearless (or who is when she's in her natural state).
zoegirl:	I stood up and waved and said, "Professor Crawford! Professor Crawford!"
SnowAngel:	um . . . why?
zoegirl:	because you were right when you told me that my prof could tell me I couldn't take the next writing class but that she couldn't keep me from writing.
SnowAngel:	I told you that?
SnowAngel:	huh. that was so smart of me! and IT IS TRUE!
zoegirl:	so I decided to tell HER that, only when she got to our booth, I totally froze.
SnowAngel:	holy shitsnacks. eeeee! nervous!

zoegirl:	I know! and if Holly and Gannon hadn't been there, I'm sure I would have totally chickened out.
zoegirl:	they've been great, by the way. it could have been weird between us, since they get to take the next class and I don't. but it isn't, because we're not letting it be.
SnowAngel:	yay! happy! but I need to know WHAT HAPPENED.
SnowAngel:	she came to your booth. you froze. and . . . ?
zoegirl:	and she stared at me like, "Can you talk?"
zoegirl:	I couldn't, it seemed, and she started to walk away. then Holly elbowed me HARD, and I said, all shakily, "I just want you to know that I won't stop writing."
SnowAngel:	Zoe!!! so proud!
SnowAngel:	what did your professor say????
zoegirl:	she got flustered. it was incredibly uncomfortable. finally she lifted her eyebrows and said, "Good."
SnowAngel:	that's all? just "good"?
zoegirl:	and *then* she walked away.
zoegirl:	it's not as if Professor Crawford is ever going to be a big part of my life, and I know I don't need her approval, but I'm glad I did it.
SnowAngel:	hell yeah! you stood up for yourself!
zoegirl:	and saying it out loud—that I'm going to keep writing no matter what—made it so that I *have* to. I said I will, so I will.
SnowAngel:	like Maddie's yolo promise . . . 😞
zoegirl:	exactly. but no sad face, because it's not over till it's over, right?
zoegirl:	and I do have another $50 for the fund. Gannon and Holly gave me $25 each.
SnowAngel:	awww, so sweet!

zoegirl:	I felt a little wrong accepting their money, but then I didn't.
SnowAngel:	Reid's going to chip in too.
SnowAngel:	we have good friends, don't we?
zoegirl:	we do. we're very lucky.
SnowAngel:	but our best friend is still in Santa Cruz in a closet somewhere. so back to it! s1

Wed, Nov 20, 1:03 PM P.S.T.

mad maddie:	hey, Zoe and Angela. stop beating yrselves up, cuz I know u are. u think it's somehow your fault that I'm going to be stuck here in California with the dorm rats and the homeless ppl, but it's not.
mad maddie:	huh
mad maddie:	I just reread that text and am now realizing that I prolly sounded . . . well, not overly convincing.
mad maddie:	just trying for gallows humor, I guess.
mad maddie:	it means SO MUCH to me that y'all even tried.
mad maddie:	and, thx to Angela, I now know that homeless ppl can make excellent friends!
mad maddie:	I will be thankful for that, and thankful that I will not be sleeping behind a dumpster like Jermaine.
mad maddie:	it's all good. really. 👍

Thu, Nov 21, 4:00 PM E.S.T.

SnowAngel:	Zoe . . . something is happening. something big and . . . strange and wonderful, and—
SnowAngel:	do you believe in miracles?
zoegirl:	sometimes. in theory.
zoegirl:	what's going on?
SnowAngel:	I know that ppl usually talk about Christmas miracles, but I'm in the middle of a Thanksgiving miracle. remember my business class and how I had to make

	a fake business? and so I made up Fashion Rescue: For the Girl on the Run!
zoegirl:	yes . . .
SnowAngel:	WELL, Lucy and Anna made up fliers and wrote testimonials and stuff. they posted them all over campus, and Anna passed them out to everyone in the Zeta house.
SnowAngel:	they know how worried I've been about Maddie, and they wanted to do something too, just like Holly and Gannon did.
SnowAngel:	and now I'm tearing up. ACK.
zoegirl:	**wait wait wait! why are you tearing up? WHAT'S GOING ON?**
SnowAngel:	also, I told Anna I was taking a VERY QUICK break— she's being, like, my set-up-appointments person— so I've gotta make this fast and get back to the next person.
SnowAngel:	we're $85 closer, Zo! I'm giving fashion advice and helping ppl reinvent themselves AND THEY'RE PAYING ME FOR IT!
zoegirl:	**no way!**
SnowAngel:	way!
SnowAngel:	thank you, Business 101! thank you, Professor Business Lady! I might even take Business 202 if there is such a thing, and grow up to be a Business Lady myself one day!!!! 😄
zoegirl:	**you're making money and you have appointments and you're a fashion consultant? I kind of think you already ARE a business lady, Angela!!!**
SnowAngel:	ooo, really? cool!
SnowAngel:	lots of my clients are Zetas, which I'm somewhat blown away by. Anna wrote "Sisters for Sisters" on the flyers she handed out at the Zeta house, and even tho I depledged, they're still helping out.

zoegirl:	all of them? even the jerky ones?
SnowAngel:	well, no. just the nice ones. but there are enough nice ones to make a difference.
SnowAngel:	they're lined up outside my room just waiting to give me money!
zoegirl:	to help Maddie?
SnowAngel:	no, to pay for the service I'm offering. (and I AM good at this stuff. every one of my clients has left happy.)
SnowAngel:	but also for Maddie, since that's what the money's for.
SnowAngel:	my heart is like a balloon, but I don't want to get Maddie's hopes up until it's for sure!
zoegirl:	wow. Angela. you are amazing!!!!
SnowAngel:	I know, right?
SnowAngel:	gtg—Anna says even more girls are lining up. they just keep coming!
zoegirl:	omg! AAAHHH!
zoegirl:	I'm going to get online and check fares again. call me when we have enough!!!

Thu, Nov 21, 6:26 PM E.S.T.

SnowAngel:	ohhhh, Maddie! we have something to tell you!
zoegirl:	it's a good something, Mads.
SnowAngel:	yeah, so are you there? say "here" if you're there.
SnowAngel:	wait. that came out wrong. if you say "here," but you are actually "there" . . .
mad maddie:	relax, I've got this.
mad maddie:	*clears throat*
mad maddie:	present. how's that?
SnowAngel:	Maddie! you answered! ★ ★ ★ ★ ★
zoegirl:	hurray! and HA, your answer made me laugh.
SnowAngel:	why laugh?
zoegirl:	from seventh grade, remember? Mrs. Rollins

	would call roll, and everyone except Maddie would say, "here." but Maddie, being Maddie, had to be different.
zoegirl:	"Angela Silver?" "Here." "Zoe Barrett?" "Here." "Madigan Kinnick?" "Present."
SnowAngel:	oh yeah! you were so weird! you've *always* been weird!
zoegirl:	but we have a REAL present for you, Mads. hee hee. 🎁
mad maddie:	**is it a turkey?**
SnowAngel:	it is not a turkey.
SnowAngel:	go check yr email.
mad maddie:	***eyes Angela and Zoe suspiciously***
mad maddie:	**if it's an e-card or something, I don't want it. not to be rude, but it wld just make things worse.**
SnowAngel:	go check yr email. we'll wait . . .
mad maddie:	**meh. grumble grumble . . .**
SnowAngel:	Mads? yr taking a loooong time. why r u taking such a long time?
zoegirl:	come back!
SnowAngel:	did she fall down?
SnowAngel:	*cups hands around mouth* Maddie! did you fall down? press the button on yr lifeline to call an ambulance!
mad maddie:	**you guys! omg, you can't do this. it's too much!**
SnowAngel:	too bad, cuz we did. 😄
zoegirl:	and it's nonrefundable, as you can see, so you're stuck.
zoegirl:	you're coming home for Thanksgiving!
mad maddie:	**omg. but . . . how'd you do it?**
SnowAngel:	ehh, we're tricky. 🙂
SnowAngel:	we'll tell u all about it in person, but right now you've got some packing to do.
zoegirl:	but are you happy? this is GOOD, Maddie, right?

mad maddie:	**are you kidding? it's fucking great! it's like . . . it's like . . .**
mad maddie:	**fuck. it's like a happily-ever-after movie ending, but this time it's real.**
mad maddie:	**and I can't even . . .**
mad maddie:	***deep breath***
SnowAngel:	it's ok. whatever it is, you can tell us.
mad maddie:	**Zoe? Angela? you two are my lifeline. and yr making me weepy, and it's pissing me off.**
SnowAngel:	yay!
SnowAngel:	weepy and pissed, but HAPPY, right?
SnowAngel:	*this* is what life is supposed to be like. this, and not any of that other crappy shit we've each had to deal with!
zoegirl:	except . . . it's all life. we can't just have the happy parts.
SnowAngel:	yes we can, because tomorrow night we are all going to be together in Atlanta!
zoegirl:	Mads, I bet you're thinking that this is great but that it's just a temporary fix. a Band-Aid.
zoegirl:	it's not, though, and I say that because YOU helped me through my dark time.
SnowAngel:	*huffs*
SnowAngel:	and I didn't?
zoegirl:	no, you did. of course you did. you were both there for me, just like we were there for you, Angela, when you pierced your foot and all that.
SnowAngel:	which is why I'm happy. 😊 we will ALWAYS be there for each other, cuz that is the law.
zoegirl:	all I'm saying is that . . . we'll figure it out. we'll soak each other in while we're in Atlanta, and it'll remind us of who we are, and we'll each go back to college a little stronger.
zoegirl:	like that girl you met on the fake "Young

Frankenstein" night. you said you met a cool girl named Morgan. was she fake too?

mad maddie: **Jordan, not Morgan, and no, she wasn't fake. she was real, and so was the fire at Taco John's and the weird boy who went "eeeee."**

zoegirl: so, you'll find Jordan again, then. or if not her, some other cool person.

SnowAngel: and Zoe's going to keep writing and maybe join the lit magazine, and I'm going to be Angelina the fashionista, AND CAN WE PLZ JUST BE HAPPY NOW?

mad maddie: **it sounds good. I'll give you that. it also sounds . . . easier said than done.**

zoegirl: so what are you saying? you're worried you're not up for the challenge?

mad maddie: **yr trying to provoke me, Zoe. don't think I can't see that.**

zoegirl: is it working?

mad maddie: **ah, screw you both. I love you two, and yes yes yes, we shld just be happy now!!!**

SnowAngel: yaaaaaay! and *I'm* not worried at all. everything will work out cuz we'll MAKE it work out.

SnowAngel: anyway, as a dear dear friend once said to me: you only live once . . . 😊

zoegirl: ha. nice, Angela.

mad maddie: **damn straight.**

mad maddie: **yolo, baby! yolo!!!**

ACKNOWLEDGMENTS

I feel so privileged—and grateful—to have been given the chance to hang out with these girls again and to celebrate the joy of friendship. To all my friends, thank you for enriching the journey in one way or another. :) To everyone at Abrams: Erica, Maria, Nicole, Jen, Maureen, Elizabeth, Jeff, Elisa, Jody, Mary, Jason, and Michael, you are all so talented at what you do, and you do it so beautifully. I am constantly humbled by your talent and forever appreciative of your hard work. Pamela, Jenny, Melyssa, Nina, and Jackie, y'all make me laugh and you let me cry, just like good friends do. My crazy family? Y'all aren't really *that* crazy, just crazy enough.

Susan, damn. How fortunate I am to move though life with you as my friend *and* my editor. There is no one finer in either regard.

Al, Jamie, and Mirabelle, all three of you light me up, and all three of you provide most excellent creative material without even knowing it.

Randy, you gave me a word-count schedule, you sent me flowers, you brought me champagne and chocolate and Moroccan stew. You support me every step of the way. You are my miracle. I love you.

LAUREN MYRACLE is the author of many books for teens and young people, including the *New York Times* bestselling Internet Girls series, *Shine*, *Rhymes with Witches*, *Bliss*, *The Infinite Moment of Us*, and the Flower Power series. She lives with her family in Fort Collins, Colorado. Visit her online at laurenmyracle.com.

A CONVERSATION WITH

LAUREN MYRACLE

What was your college like? Was your college most like UGA, Kenyon, or UCSC?

I went to the University of North Carolina at Chapel Hill. I *wanted* to go to the University of California at Santa Cruz, but after getting accepted, and after the due dates for financial aid had passed (without my applying for aid), my dad said, "Sorry, Lauren, I'm not going to pay for you to go to California. California is too wild for you." My dad has grown since then! So have I. Also, who said he had to pay for me to go to college at all, right? But with self-sabotaging 17-year-old logic, I said, "FINE. Then I'll go to the dumb school YOU want me to go to." (Which was Chapel Hill—which is NOT a dumb school.) Anyway. Which of the Winsome Threesome's schools was UNC most like? UGA, I guess . . . ? Big southern state university???

What was a highlight from your college experience? What was a low point for you?

Highlight? Everything bagels with veggie cream cheese from a bagel place on the main drag. Low point? Well, almost every-thing else. I SUCKED AT COLLEGE. I got great grades—don't get me wrong. But I was LOST and sad and lonely in such a huge school, and I felt very different from the other students there. I would do better if given a second shot. Still, I should've gone to Kenyon, where Zoe went, instead.

What about the girls' experiences in college can you relate to the most?

Like Zoe: Being told in my introductory creative writing class that I wasn't good enough to move on to the next level.

Like Maddie: Feeling like a loser for not having fun while all my other friends were relaying great stories of hijinks, hilarity, and hot guys.

Like Angela: Hmm. I went through rush, like Angela, and, like Angela, I decided not to pledge. BUT I also saw that the Greek world is multifaceted. Not pure good, not pure evil. Duh, I know—but it was another stereotype that broke down for me through personal experience.

College shapes Maddie, Zoe, and Angela in some unexpected ways. Angela discovers her business savvy, Maddie no longer feels like "the wild one," and Zoe is able to break out of her "good girl" mold a bit. Did you also find that college changed you as a person?

Yes. It made me feel like a big loser. See above. :) But, honestly, being lonely is not a terrible thing to live through—as long as you come out on the other side. I took great solace in books (as always). I took bowling as an elective—and I rocked it! And I saw all of these (mainly) awesome professors with careers they loved, and it reinforced my determination to have a career that *I* loved. The fact that I got booted out of the creative writing program helped with that, too. It sucked. Don't get me wrong. But after crying quietly in the children's section of Chapel Hill's public library, which is where I ran to hide after my professor told me, in front of the whole class, that "perhaps writing wasn't for [me]," I wiped my face off and pledged to myself that I would STILL be a writer, damn it, and that that professor could go suck an egg.

It's been eight years since *l8r, g8r* was published. What was it like to revisit these characters after that gap in time?

Awwww. So fun. Love those girls. THEY were the same, but their technology had changed! That was the biggest difference. It was hard/fun/challenging to update the first three books by giving the girls easy texting options, smart phones, etc. Then, in *yolo*, the technology was incorporated far more organically. It was a fun challenge.

Any roommate stories, good or bad?

Hahahahaha. My first roommate refused to look at herself in a mirror unless she'd already applied her makeup. So she applied her makeup by candlelight, then turned on the overhead light to do last-minute touch-ups. Also, she had never looked at her vagina in her life, she told me. Ever. And she didn't plan to.

What would be your advice to someone just starting out in college?

Oh, honey-honeys, FIND A COMMUNITY! Make yourself! Join a frickin' club, or a sorority, or whatever. Sit down next to non-creepy strangers and TALK to them. They're probably nervous, too. And take classes that stretch your conception of what you think you like or are good at. Oh! And for heaven's sake, don't be practical. Major in what you LOVE and never give up your dreams!!!!!!!!

"Last Friday Night (T.G.I.F.)" by Katy Perry

"Boom Clap" by Charli XCX

"The Motto" by Drake, Lil Wayne

"Shut Up and Dance" by Walk the Moon

"Brave" by Sara Bareilles

"Girls Chase Boys" by Ingrid Michaelson

"California" by Phantom Planet

"Someone Like You" by Adele

"Stay Alive" by Jose Gonzalez

"The Cave" by Mumford & Sons

"Pictures of You" by The Cure

"Don't Save Me" by Haim

"Comeback Kid (That's My Dog)" by Brett Dennen

"Rather Be" by Clear Bandit, featuring Jess Glynne

NEW YORK TIMES BESTSELLER

LAUREN MYRACLE

ttfn

Through texts and messages, three best friends
share the highs and lows of high school.

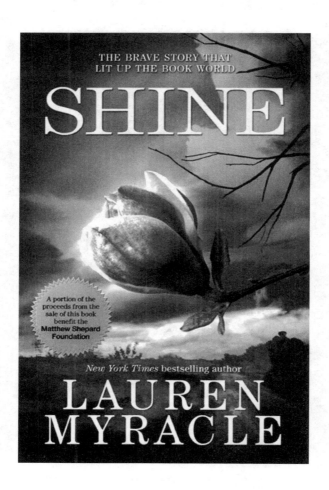